PENGU...
TWENTY-NINE G... ...HIRTY

Andaleeb Wajid has published thirteen novels, of which three are e-books. Her young adult novel *When She Went Away* was shortlisted for The Hindu Young World-Goodbooks Awards 2017. Andaleeb enjoys writing about food, and her most popular novel is *More than Just Biryani*, a book about food and love. She is a full-time writer and a creative writing facilitator at Nutcracker Workshops.

ADVANCE PRAISE FOR THE BOOK

'Wajid writes everyday tales with empathy, subtle humour and an acute sense of storytelling. *Twenty-nine Going on Thirty* is a compelling, heart-warming tale of growing up when you're already grown-up.' —Kiran Manral, author of *All Aboard!*

'Wajid's writing is warm, witty and wonderful!'—Anuja Chandramouli, author of the Yama's Lieutenant series

'Fantastically funny and brilliant. One of the most entertaining romances I've read in a while.'—Bilal Siddiqi, author of *The Bard of Blood* and *The Stardust Affair*

'Office politics, fast friends, meddling parents, crippling crushes, messy relationships . . . Wajid captures all the angst and romance of being twenty-nine going on thirty.'—Aruna Nambiar, author of *Mango Cheeks, Metal Teeth*

'Wajid's world is of the sparkly and brilliant, of extraordinary drama in ordinary lives. Dishy neighbours, spazzed-out friends and vacuous colleagues add to this mishmash of delectable storytelling.'—Nandita Bose, author of *Tread Softly*

'A savvy take on the lives of modern working women balancing it all—office, family, romance and the angst of ageing. Breezy, humorous and entertaining.'—Sajita Nair, author of *She's a Jolly Good Fellow*

'It's as real as it gets. You almost want to go next door or peer into the next cubicle and check in on Priya and the gang and partake in the drama. Wajid has captured the essence of what life is like for working, turning-thirty-year-old women in India today. Her characters are as real, funny and eye-rollingly dramatic as turning thirty is.' —Khushnuma Daruwala, author of *50 Cups of Coffee*

'Wajid is at the top of her game here as she spins a love story—make that three-and-a-half love stories—which closely entangles hot males, sassy females and the non-magical age of thirty. One very enjoyable read!'—Sheila Kumar, author of *No Strings Attached*

'Enthralling. Captivating. I devoured it in one sitting. Wajid makes us believe that you do not have to be of a certain age to find love and happiness in your life. It can come to you any time.'—Sara Naveed, author of *Our Story Ends Here*

Twenty-nine going on Thirty

Andaleeb Wajid

PENGUIN BOOKS

An imprint of Penguin Random House

PENGUIN BOOKS

USA | Canada | UK | Ireland | Australia
New Zealand | India | South Africa | China

Penguin Books is part of the Penguin Random House group of companies
whose addresses can be found at global.penguinrandomhouse.com

Published by Penguin Random House India Pvt. Ltd
7th Floor, Infinity Tower C, DLF Cyber City,
Gurgaon 122 002, Haryana, India

First published in Penguin Books by Penguin Random House India 2018

Copyright © Andaleeb Wajid 2018

10 9 8 7 6 5 4 3 2 1

ISBN 9780143441182

Typeset in Adobe Garamond Pro by Manipal Digital Systems, Manipal
Printed at Replika Press Pvt. Ltd, India

www.penguin.co.in

1

'Nobody should bring their family dramas to work,' I tell the three youngsters sitting in front of me, catching one in the middle of rolling her eyes not so surreptitiously.

'But permanent employees can?' cheeky Amrita, constant eye-roller, asks.

'No, not even them,' I say, trying to look as if I don't know what they're talking about.

'Um, we just overheard you fight with your mother on the phone,' Ayaz pipes in.

Bloody interns; think no end of themselves. I look over at the third intern, Namrata, who is staring into the distance dreamily. If it weren't for the way she dressed and her background (which the HR very unhelpfully whispered about into my ears when she first joined), I'd bet she was stoned. But no. She's apparently just daydreaming. I try to temper my irritation because she's such a sweet girl. I envy her clear dusky skin, but the way she hides her face in her hair all the time is getting to be annoying. She always ties it up in a loose braid that hangs over her shoulders and nearly reaches her waist. She has a front parting, and the sloping sides cover half her face, which is intentional I think.

'Namrata!' I call out loudly, causing her to jerk awake.

'Yes! Yes, Priya. We'll take care of it,' she says.

Ayaz and Amrita snigger, and I flash a look at them. Take it easy on her, I try to convey to them with a meaningful raise of my eyebrow.

'Dude, you need to change your beauty salon. Something is wrong with your eyebrow,' Amrita says.

Dude? Seriously? I'm supposed to be their boss. I have that momentary confusion where I don't know if I'm thrilled they think of me as 'dude' or affronted that they don't give me the respect that's due to me. I'd called the three of them to the conference room for an impromptu meeting to explain the newest campaign that I was planning to launch but had been sidetracked by my mother's phone call.

The conference room door opens and a dark head peeps in.

'Fuck. This room is also taken. Let's check the next one,' a husky voice announces. The owner of the dark head and husky voice is Mini, who confidently flouts the company's dress code. I admire her for it, but also know I can never pull it off. People will think I'm sick and dying, or acting out; while Mini, forever dressed in black, hair cut in an extreme Goth style, with her silver nose ring, dark eyeliner, dark eyeshadow and even dark lipstick, really pulls off the look, making her the most stunning girl I've ever seen.

There's silence in the wake of her exit and everyone is still staring at the door as if she will return any moment. I clear my throat and all three of them reluctantly turn back to me.

Mini just seems to have that effect on everyone. People pause in the middle of whatever they're doing to look at her as she walks by. I've seen her show the staring people her middle finger as she crosses them, and although people try hard not to look at her again, they just can't seem to help themselves.

'I want to grow up and be her,' Amrita sighs.

'Why is she working here? She . . .'

'Is a brilliant coder and that's why she's here,' I finish Ayaz's sentence. 'Now, I know only one of you will stay on by the end of the month, but I'd like all of you to at least put in some effort. You know I have to report to the HR about your performance.'

'Yeah, yeah,' Amrita says, getting up from the table. 'Don't be such an aunty about it.' Realizing that this probably sounded too arrogant, she quickly flashes me a smile that is half simpering and half mocking, and fully fake.

I glare at her. Aunty. How dare she. Namrata gets up to follow them and smiles at me weakly. I immediately decide that at the end of the month, I'm going to retain Namrata and let the other two go, even if it means holding her hand for every bloody thing.

Being the team lead of the social media marketing department isn't half as fancy as it sounds, considering I'm the only person in the team. But then, that's a recent occurrence. Two of my team members quit suddenly, leaving me alone to manage the ship.

I'm responsible for the company's outward-facing image on social media. Citron, the company I work for, is a product-based software company in Bangalore. It wants to croon about the benefits of its accounting product to potential customers without hitting them over the head with it. So, I have to constantly think of new campaigns with blog posts and webinars that would direct people to our company website and eventually convert into sales.

Recently, I have been assigned three interns, and the HR has told me to try and retain one of them for my team because I obviously can't do everything on my own. Of course, Citron is cutting corners by giving me interns because they cost considerably less, although we would need to spend a significant amount of time training them. Considering Amrita's and Ayaz's attitudes, I know I'm making a good decision in choosing Namrata.

It's Monday, 11.30 a.m., and my head feels like it's going to split in two already. My mother has been on my case all morning on the phone and I had to end the call when I reached the office. But she called again. Honestly, that woman has no boundaries.

'Haan, but you're turning thirty this year, ma,' she said, as though I needed reminding. I gritted my teeth to stop myself from snapping at her, and, without realizing, smiled manically at the hot new guy, Vinay, who joined a couple of months ago. I swear he shuddered. Nevertheless, I don't need my mom reminding me of my age.

I'm twenty-nine. For another sixty days. I'm on the cusp of falling into the dreaded pit of thirty—when kids like Amrita and Ayaz will be justified in calling me an aunty. When I'll start wearing cotton bras because they breathe better; when my mom will send pictures of men who everyone else has rejected, hoping that someone will catch my eye; when I'll have to tick the 'thirty–forty years' box whenever I fill forms or take surveys.

God, my life is over.

2

'I wish I were you,' I tell Farida during lunch. She laughs loudly, the sound amplifying on the phone.

'I mean, look at you. You don't have to dress up and come to work and face bratty interns who think you're aunty material. You can stay at home in your PJs, paint or laze around,' I tell her fervently.

'Please. I've told you to quit that job like a hundred times already,' she drawls.

'And do what? I need to pay rent,' I tell her.

'Um, I've told you many times, I can pay it but you don't listen,' she protests. Farida lives with me and pays a huge chunk of my rent because she comes from a rich family. Her parents died in an accident when we were in school and her foster family managed to *kabza maaro* her house. She recently ran away when her slimy foster uncle tried to molest her and came to live with me. She still gets paid a hefty allowance every month because her parents made sure she was well-provided-for. She's offered to pay my entire rent, but I refuse to let her because it wouldn't be right.

'No, even if it weren't for the rent, I can't stay at home doing nothing. I don't know anything other than social media marketing. I don't have any defining talent. I'm not like you,' I tell her, putting the phone between my ear and shoulder as I grab a plate from the buffet line.

'Priya Kumar, you don't have to paint or be a photographer like moi,' she says in a soothing voice.

'Haan, but there is literally nothing else I can do,' I tell her as the server dumps a ladleful of white rice on my plate even though I shake my head, indicating that I don't want it. I was angling for the chapatti but then people behind me nudge me forward and before I can say anything, he drowns the rice in rasam and sambar and plops some sort of unidentifiable vegetable on the side.

I look at my plate in dismay and tell Farida I'll call her back in a minute. But the phone slips from my shoulder, slides down my chest and lands on the plate with a plop.

Amrita and Ayaz, who are eating at a table not too far away and have been observing everything, burst out laughing at the shocked expression on my face. Noooo! Not another phone!

Thankfully, Namrata, who is standing right behind me, quickly grabs the phone from the midst of the food and dabs at it somewhat ineffectively with tissues. The server, who looks like the most bored man on the planet, rocks forward and backwards on his heels, impatiently indicating I should move on.

I pick up the mandatory sweet of the day, gulab jamun in a plastic cup (I mean, yes, my phone fell into a plate of rasam and sambar, so why should I leave the only thing worth eating here?) and walk away; Namrata is behind me, still holding on to my phone.

I find a place to sit and then inspect the phone, hoping I wouldn't have to buy another one again. I mean, the last one was just three months ago, when I accidentally knocked it off the top of the flush tank into the lavatory bowl.

I'm not a klutz, but I just have these momentary lapses when something or the other goes wrong and it usually ends up with me having to shell out ten to fifteen thousand on a new phone.

'Thank god I didn't listen to Farida and buy an iPhone,' I mutter to myself and then realize that Namrata is sitting beside me, smiling somewhat vacantly.

'Hey, um, maybe you should start eating,' I tell her, gesturing towards her plate with my head while shaking droplets of rasam from my phone. Please switch on. Please switch on.

The rasam-stained display stubbornly refuses to come on. I exhale loudly and look up to see Amrita and Ayaz mimicking me and collapsing into giggles. And then, just as suddenly, they stop. It's like a black cloud has passed over them.

Mini.

She's looking for a place to sit, and I'm pretty sure those two awestruck idiots would have offered their own seats if they had remembered to stop gawking, think and actually say something.

She looks around, spots the empty seat across from me and plonks herself down. Namrata, like everyone else, is a little intimidated by her.

'Ruined yet another phone,' I tell Mini conversationally with a grim smile.

'I'm sorry. What?' she asks, narrowing her eyes. Up close, her eyes are gorgeous. Luminous, with thick lashes; and her eyeliner is like a work of art. You can stare at her eyes forever.

'Dropped my phone into my plate,' I tell her and she looks at me, at the phone and then goes back to eating. I can sense people are looking at our table because she's there. I wonder how she feels about this constant scrutiny, this constant need people have to stare at her.

Suddenly, I'm overcome with compassion for her but I don't know what to say. And much as I hate to admit it, I'm a little scared of her myself.

'Why isn't she eating?' Mini says, indicating Namrata with her spoon. Namrata, who has been staring into the distance, hasn't heard her. She can't possibly daydream so much, I think, looking in the direction she's staring.

Oh.

She's been staring at Vinay all this while. Oh, you poor thing. Vinay is the male version of Mini in Citron, except that he has more than just black in his wardrobe. Everyone stares at him too but, thankfully, he's not rude and brash like her. He's immensely likeable and friendly, and he can't help being the way he looks. He's tall and ripped. For software engineers who are constantly sitting on their asses, he's an aberration. And he's not even a dumb jock. He's articulate and well spoken, and very much taken, a fact we're reminded of when his girlfriend Radhika puts her hand on his broad shoulders in an unmistakably intimate way as she walks around his table and sits down across from him, somewhat blocking our view.

Apparently, the HR manager had a long talk with them because inter-office romance is not encouraged, even though

Radhika and Vinay work on different projects. But Vinay's earnest charm won over our stuffy manager and he winked and told Vinay he was looking forward to the wedding. Of course, that was not what Vinay had expected. In fact, if the water cooler and ladies' room gossip is accurate, things are not fine between the hottest couple in office.

Even so, Namrata doesn't stand a chance, I think instinctively, and then feel guilty about such thoughts. Mini, who has finished eating by now, gets up, holding her plate. As she turns around, she glances at Vinay. I pick up my glass of water and wish it were something stronger in which I could drown my misery, to make me forget the expense and headache of getting a new phone.

'Such an extremely fuckable chap,' Mini comments as she walks away. The water goes down the wrong pipe and I choke and sputter while Namrata, who is blushing, pats my back awkwardly. It's not the comment that shocks me but the fact that she said it out here where any number of our prudish colleagues can hear her and probably report her to the HR manager.

Knowing Mini, she'd probably tell them to fuck off, too.

3

Peanut butter is one of my weaknesses. A lot of people think that's weird. Farida goes on and on about Nutella, but someone give me a jar of peanut butter and I'll lick it clean. Even better if I can somehow combine it with chocolate. I know how this sounds for my cholesterol, but I can't bring myself to stop. It's not like Nutella is perfect either.

Given the crappy day I've had, I really need some of the magical stuff. I park my scooter in the basement and head to the nearby store to pick out the smallest jar of peanut butter I can find. As I enter the store, I remember that living on my own doesn't mean I can buy only things to fix my mood. There are boring things like dhania powder, salt and jeera powder that Parvati akka, our cook, has been harassing me to get.

Feeling domesticated, I add those things to my basket and then remember even more stuff I need. Aargh. What's a person to do to indulge in their mood fixer here? Why did I have to remember that my face wash was over and I'd run out of sanitary napkins?

Now, I'm just feeling murderous. It could just be the onset of PMS but sometimes it feels like it's always there. Nevertheless, I fill the basket, head to the checkout counter and pay the bill. The guy at the counter narrows his eyes when he sees I don't have a bag with me to carry my purchases.

'Madam, no plastic bags,' he says, pointing to the sign behind him, which says that customers have to bring their own bags.

I just came here for peanut butter which could have easily gone into my handbag. I ended up buying all this shit instead.

'I'll pay for a bag,' I tell him and he shakes his head in an annoying manner.

'We don't keep any bags,' he announces. Does this mean I have to carry all these things in my hand now, I think furiously. I'm tempted to dump everything except the peanut butter when, from behind me, a hand slides forward with a cloth bag.

'I have an extra bag. You can use it,' the owner of the hand says. The cashier starts dumping everything in it. I turn around to thank my saviour and realize I'm staring at a broad chest instead of a face.

I look up and stare into the warmest brown eyes I've ever seen. Seriously. They are like caramel candy. The face they peer out of is also nice. Not in a chiselled sort of way but altogether very attractive.

'Thank you so much!' I tell him with a smile, and he smiles back. One crooked tooth in the bottom row adds to his charm, and I feel a fluttering in my stomach as a warm tingle spreads over me.

'You're welcome,' he says and motions with his head to move. Feeling slightly idiotic for gawping at him like that, I step aside and let him pay for his stuff. I know I should turn around and leave. I should go home. Peanut butter is waiting for me.

But I stand there pretending to check something on my phone (which is, of course, not functioning) and surreptitiously look at the items he's checking out. He must have fantastic metabolism, I wonder enviously as I note the amount of junk food he's buying and sneak a look at him too. He looks extremely fit in his white T-shirt and jeans. Nice, lean arms, and good-looking hands, I think. I straighten up and turn to leave because I realize the cashier is glancing at me.

'Do you live nearby?' he asks. The bag guy, not the cashier.

I turn around slightly; not sure I want to tell him where I live, so I smile weakly. He's tall, has nice hair that's turning the slightest bit grey and the nicest smile, really. There are a number of little things about him that hit me right away but I can't pinpoint them individually because the total effect is so mesmerizing.

When I don't reply, he shakes his head as he lifts his bag in the air and nods towards the apartment building nearby. My apartment building.

'We moved in just yesterday,' he says.

Oh. We.

I smile and nod, still not willing to tell him I live there too. We walk out together as he continues talking to me, unaware that mentally I have just marked him off my non-existent list of good-looking, well-spoken and eligible men.

'Would you believe that one five-year-old can eat all this crap?' he muses while walking towards the building. I merely smile in reply.

'I leave her with my wife's family for fifteen days. Fifteen days. That's it. I come back from the US and she's turned into this junk food eating machine,' he exclaims. He seems to have realized I'm following him, probably looking like a lost puppy.

At the ground floor foyer, near the lift, he looks at me, somewhat embarrassed. He nods to me. 'I live here,' he says as he jabs the lift button with a finger.

I smile and nod. 'So do I,' I tell him and push aside the scissor gates to enter the lift. To say that his face lights up at the announcement is an understatement. He enters and pushes the scissor gates until they close with a clang. We both end up pressing the button for the third floor.

'No! You live on the same floor!' he says beaming.

'Yup. For the past five years now,' I tell him. His enthusiasm and happiness are catchy until I remember he has a wife and a daughter. The lift creaks and groans as it moves up and I look down, not wanting to meet his eyes.

I look up when the lift stops and realize he's been staring at me. There's a funny look in his eyes but he doesn't say anything.

We both end up trying to pull the gates open. I step back and let him do it because when his fingers land on mine, I feel a swooping sensation in my stomach.

'Thanks for the bag!' I tell him as I walk towards my door at the end of the corridor. I fish out my key from my handbag and turn it in the lock. When I turn slightly, he's still there!

He smiles and waves at me before heading into 303 which is across the corridor, closer to the lift. I nod politely and push open my door.

4

'What are the odds?' I ask Farida a little later as I scrape the last bit of peanut butter from the jar with a spoon and bring it to my mouth.

'Very high odds actually,' she says, as she gets up from the sofa where she's been watching TV all this while.

'What do you mean?' I turn to her and lean forward to place the now empty jar of peanut butter on the centre table.

'When is anything perfect? You meet a nice guy, turns out he's married. It's a good thing you got to know that at the outset, right? And imagine how messy it would be even if he was single? I mean, if dating co-workers is a no-no, then what about dating neighbours? That's even worse, I would think,' she shudders.

I let out a sigh. My stomach protests the slightest bit in the background. 'You're jumping the gun. No one is dating any neighbour. But such a . . . a . . .' I realize I don't actually have words to describe him. He's not hot like Vinay but there's so much charm—that smile for one. He has managed to check off all the right boxes for me. He is tall, has a nice physique and broad shoulders. Those caramel-candy eyes make him

14

look youthful, despite the greying hair. And that smile with his one adorable crooked tooth . . . I sigh. I need to get a grip on myself.

I notice that Farida has already tuned out and is looking out of the window at the children who are playing in the sultry June evening in the nearby park. Remembering that I have to buy a new phone, I pull out my laptop from its case and open it.

'Come and help me buy a new phone,' I call out to her.

'Nah. You do it,' she says. I frown. That's very unlike her. New phones and gadgets are like candy for her. She finds them irresistible. Every time I buy a new phone, she usually takes it away from me, fiddles with it and checks it out thoroughly before giving it back.

'Everything okay?' I ask, even as I open the website.

She doesn't reply but continues staring out the window.

'Hello? Farida? All okay?' I ask her, shutting my laptop and walking up to her. The kids in the park are all going back home reluctantly.

She turns to me and sighs loudly, shaking her head. 'Reshma Phuppu came here today.'

'What?' I look at her outraged. 'How did she get past the watchman? Haven't we told him not to let her in?'

Farida shrugs and turns away from the window. 'I don't know how she sneaked past him, but I opened the door and there she was. I tried shutting the door in her face but she just barged in and started shouting.' Farida winces at the memory.

'Shit. Then? Why didn't you call me?' I ask.

'I did. But your phone was out of commission by then. Anyway, I managed it,' she says, looking troubled.

'Right. My phone,' I say, shutting my eyes in regret for a second. 'But how did you manage to kick her out?'

When she doesn't say anything, I know what she's done.

'How much?' I ask her angrily.

'Twenty,' she says, looking downcast.

I gasp. 'But didn't she already get her monthly pay-off from you?' I can't understand the dynamics between Farida and this woman, her aunt. She's supposed to be Farida's father's cousin who showed up after her parents died. Since Farida was just thirteen then, it seemed serendipitous to let the woman help out. The timing of her appearance was suspicious, but at the time we didn't know we wouldn't be able to get rid of her. Also, Farida is too much of a bleeding heart to kick out a relative.

'Yes, she did. But she says her husband needs money for some surgery . . .' Farida stops as her entire body shudders. Yuck. Reshma Phuppu's husband is the reason why Farida has been living with me for the past year now. He's one slimy character. With his slouchy posture and pitted skin, he'll win no awards in a beauty pageant. But his small shifty eyes and dandruff just make everything worse. He is always either scratching his head or some other part of his body. He tried getting into Farida's room one night, which was the reason she ran from her own house and moved in with me. But the downside of it was that her 'relatives' now refuse to leave the house.

'What we need is a good lawyer,' I tell her as I open my laptop and hover over phone choices. She sighs and comes and sits next to me, narrowing her eyes critically at my options.

'Yeah. Forget it. I don't want to talk about her. You know, you should probably buy one of those old Nokia phones. They're perfect for you,' she says.

'Ha ha. Very funny,' I tell her as I look at the features of the one I'm fairly certain I'll buy.

'Speaking of phones, aunty called me,' she says, and I look at her in dismay.

'I already spoke to her twice today. What does she want? And why did you wait until now to tell me?'

'Well, you came home all abuzz with excitement about meeting a cute guy who happens to live on our floor and I didn't want to ruin your moment,' she says, taking my laptop from me and putting it on her lap.

'What did she want?' I ask, throwing my arm over my eyes dramatically.

'To know why you weren't answering your phone,' she says with a grin.

5

As I leave for the office the next morning, I'm wary about bumping into our new neighbour. I don't want to like him too much. But apparently, fate is not on my side. I find him outside his door, locking it, looking slightly dishevelled as he hitches the strap of his laptop bag on to his shoulder.

He looks at me and shakes his head. 'First day of school for Anya, and we messed everything up. Woke up late, realized I'd made her wear the uniform which is only to be worn on Fridays and she didn't want breakfast. Uff,' he says tiredly as he finally locks his door.

I smile uncertainly. 'Where's she now?' I ask, because I certainly don't see any five-year-olds around.

'That's what I was telling you. I dropped her off at school and came back to get ready. It's my first day at work at a new place too,' he says. I nod politely and make my way towards the lift. He watches me push the scissor gates open and shakes his head again.

'I bet the stairs are faster. Bet's on. Loser has to buy the winner coffee this evening,' he says as he sprints down the steps two at a time before I can say anything. Inside the lift,

I'm not amused. Of course, he's going to get there before me, and I don't want to have coffee with him. He's too affable and charming, and also very married. What's wrong with men these days, I wonder.

Fuming, I get out of the lift in the dark basement, ready to lash out at him but, of course, he's not hanging around waiting for me. He's already in his car and backing out as I make my way towards my scooter.

'Coffee this evening then,' he says with a smile. I don't smile back, but he's already left with a wave of his hand. So presumptuous of him, I think, as I get myself ready to face the Bangalore traffic on a two-wheeler.

By the time I emerge from the basement, my face is swathed in a dupatta that I keep expressly for this purpose, and a helmet covers my head. Only my eyes can be seen. I fix my sunglasses on my face, ensuring that they sit perfectly, and leave. I know that I probably look like a hipster Egyptian mummy with an inflated head but I refuse to breathe the polluted air even though I'm suffocating in the June heat.

Once I reach my office parking lot on the ground floor, I quickly peel off the dupatta and stash it in my scooter's storage space. Once upstairs, I swipe my card at the entrance and head straight towards the restroom to freshen up and make sure my hair can be made to look normal. I quickly wash my hands, brush my hair and look at myself in the mirror critically. I'm still thinking about my neighbour (I don't even know his name yet) and wondering if he's as attracted to me as I am to him. It's a downward spiral, going down this road, because I know I'll waste a good ten minutes staring at the mirror and I'll have to call Farida to give me a reality check since he's married and has a little girl.

But now that I've begun, I can't help it. Maybe . . . he likes girls with long wavy hair, I think as I brush my hair carefully. Or maybe it's the eyes—nowhere near as dramatic as Mini's or even as elegantly almond-shaped as Farida's. I know many people have said that I have expressive eyes, whatever that means. I turn my body sideways. The office ladies' room mirror is not full-length, just half, so I can't see the rest of my body. I'm average-sized, neither too thin nor too fat. But I have nice shapely arms, I think, as I turn a little and examine them in the mirror. It's one of the reasons why I love wearing sleeveless outfits.

I'm brought back to reality when I hear sniffling sounds from the restroom stall, without Farida needing to kick sense into me.

Should I leave? I'm sure the person in the stall will be embarrassed to find me outside. But before I can put my brush back in my bag and hurry out, the door opens.

Mini steps out, her nose red, eyes looking like a raccoon's as all her black make-up is smeared everywhere. She stares at me balefully and then moves to the sink to wash her face. Silently, I offer her a tube of face wash from my bag, and she proceeds to lather up her face and wash it all off.

She splashes her face with water and I can sense a little of the real Mini emerging from underneath her usual make-up. I pull out a couple of tissues from the dispenser and hand her a bottle of moisturizer to remove the eye make-up that is still quite evident.

She shakes her head, refusing my offer of help and braces her arms against the sink, looking into the mirror. I turn to leave when she calls out again.

'Priya,' she says, her voice huskier than usual because of her crying bout. I turn around, surprised she even knows my name. I look at her outstretched hand for a second, not understanding and then quickly realize that she wants the moisturizer and tissues.

She begins removing her eye make-up and by the time she's done, she looks like she's fifteen. Her face is a little splotchy and she doesn't look like the stunner she is normally. But you wouldn't consider her plain either. I can still see those high cheekbones that her make-up usually accentuates. And her eyes are beautiful, even without the eyeliner and kohl.

'Thanks,' she mutters and lets out a deep breath. I leave, wondering what could have caused her to cry. Normally, as she succinctly says, she doesn't give a flying fuck about anything.

In my work bay later, I look around, hoping to spot her but instead notice Namrata mooning over Vinay again. I grab her hand, pull her towards me, wheeling a chair along, and sit her down.

Then I completely lose my train of thought. What am I thinking? Who am I to give her a talking-to? Err, her boss? How can I be cruel enough to tell her to stop dreaming about Vinay because he's so completely out of her league?

'Namrata, I'll be handing in my reports to the HR manager this Friday and I want you to know that I plan on retaining you. But you're going to have to change your game,' I tell her instead.

She looks completely awake and even blinks a little,
probably from surprise. She straightens up and smiles. 'Thank
you so much, Priya. You won't regret it,' she says.

I exhale loudly. 'Yes, but you need to stay focused on
work,' I tell her, stressing the last word. Of course, she doesn't
get my hint and looks puzzled. I don't want to say it outright,
though.

'Yes, I'll stay focused on work,' she repeats my words to
me. She's looking at me but I can sense her struggle to avoid
looking in the periphery of her vision where Vinay is talking
to Radhika earnestly. Radhika's team sits on our floor, near
our bay actually, and it's the reason why we see so much of
Vinay.

'Vinay and Radhika make such a good-looking couple,
no?' I ask her and her face falls at the reminder that the guy
she has a crush on is very obviously taken.

6

Not having a phone for a legitimate reason is actually liberating, as I have observed every few months when I've destroyed the old one and am waiting for the new one to arrive. I always tell myself that I will be less dependent on my phone in the future and be more focused on the world around me. That resolution lasts only until I get the shiny new cell phone in my hands.

Nevertheless, today promises to be relaxing because there's no way my mother can reach out to me. I spoke to her yesterday on Farida's phone and assured her that I will be getting a new mobile soon. Her incredulity knew no bounds when she heard that I'd managed to ruin yet another one.

So, without the phone to turn to during bouts of boredom in the office, I've managed not just to get a lot of work done but also to be clued into what's happening. The office grapevine, which is not often the most accurate source of information, tells me that Mini had a terrible break-up with her boyfriend, which was most likely the reason why I saw her crying in the ladies' room.

I'm pretty gobsmacked. I had no idea she had a boyfriend. She looks like she eats men for breakfast and spits them out if they don't suit her. Clearly, the relationship meant a lot to her. But she was so secretive about it, it's a wonder that anyone in the office even found out about the break-up.

Apparently, she was talking tearfully on the phone in the ladies' room, begging some guy not to leave her, when someone overheard her. Naturally, whoever it was didn't care for her privacy and soon everyone knew about Mini's break-up.

I feel rather outraged on her behalf, and want to talk to her and help her feel better, but I'm wary of approaching her when she's like this. Also, she went home early today, in fact right before lunch, probably because she didn't want to face anyone. I don't blame her. Office gossip can be nasty and she's already the centre of attention for just being the way she is.

I'm done for the day. My back is aching from being hunched over the laptop all day as I worked out a schedule for the new campaign. I had to decide who was going to write which article and who would record the webinar. For the past three months it's been just me, which has been all kinds of hectic. The interns have been a mixed blessing. I finally have someone to lean on, but then, I also have to train them every step of the way, which can be a big headache.

I'm about to head home when Namrata approaches me with a doubt about something. Namrata's writing is much better than Amrita's or Ayaz's, although I had to introduce her to search engine optimization (SEO) and keep reminding her to use the keywords given by the SEO team. I wonder what she's done this time as I take her to the nearest conference room to talk in private, and run smack into Vinay, who looks embarrassed for some reason as he ends a call on his phone. Namrata freezes and gawks at him while he ignores her and gives me a pained smile as he exits.

I wonder what that was all about. Namrata and I enter the conference room and I feel I might as well go home because Namrata seems to have forgotten all about her question. She looks lost as she sits down, and I glare at her in exasperation.

'Are we going to discuss this matter or not?' I ask her. She looks at me and shakes her head.

'Fine. I'm going then,' I tell her but she stops me.

'Do you have an extra room in your apartment?' she asks.

'What?'

She looks extremely embarrassed and shakes her head vigorously. 'S-sorry I asked. I don't know what I was thinking,' she says, covering her face with her trembling hands.

I sit back and stare at her for a moment.

'Is there a problem at home?' I ask because I remember what the HR manager told me about her family situation. Her father died when she was young, and her mother brought up Namrata and her brother by herself. Her mother worked as a domestic help and made sure they got a good education. Her brother got a job and things were fine for them until he got married. His wife didn't like Namrata and his mother staying with them and constantly made their lives miserable. For one, she stopped Namrata's brother from giving them money.

Namrata is a distant relative of our HR manager, which was how she got the internship. It's also the reason I know so much about her life. I could have really done without all these details, believe me, but the HR manager insisted on telling me the whole story.

She looks miserable. 'I don't know. I want to leave home but I can't because I don't have any money. The internship stipend is barely enough to cover my travel expenses. All my money from my previous jobs went to my mother and she used it to run our home. I don't want to leave my mother alone with my brother and sister-in-law, who's always nagging us or looking for ways to make us unhappy,' she says.

I nod in silence at first and then realize what she's said. 'Previous jobs? What previous jobs?' I ask incredulously.

'I used to work as a content writer in a media house,' she says.

'What?'

'And before that I worked as a teacher in my old college for a bit. I taught metaphysical poetry. I loved that job but the pay was too little.'

To say that I'm stunned is an understatement.

'You were a college lecturer? When? How old are you?' I ask her. She looks like she just finished college . . . and I assumed she was the same age as Amrita and Ayaz, my other two interns.

She looks slightly abashed. 'I'm turning thirty this year,' she says.

'Get out of here!' I tell her shocked. Unfortunately, she takes me literally and stands up, her eyes filling with tears.

'No, no! I didn't mean it that way. Sit down. I had no idea you were the same age as me,' I mutter and she sits back, looking slightly suspiciously at me through teary eyes.

'Unfortunately, I don't have an extra room in my apartment right now. My friend Farida is staying with me and she has her own set of issues because of which she can't go back home. But I'll keep an eye out for places where you can stay. We'll get you moved out of there soon,' I assure her.

She looks stricken for some reason and shakes her head. 'No . . . I'll stay in my house. You said you were going to confirm my position here. Maybe once I have more money, things will be better,' she says.

I stare at her for a while in silence. I knew she had problems at home but didn't know they were this bad.

'You can come to me if you need anything,' I assure her. 'And I will still keep an eye out for flats or people looking for flatmates.'

She thanks me quietly and gets up to leave, while I sit for a bit, thinking about her. Namrata's life is so messy and complicated, compared to some of us who bitch about our lives just because EMIs take away more than half our salaries. Then, there's her evident crush on Vinay, something of a bright spot in her life. Imagine what she'd feel like if she knew he's twenty-seven? I decide not to tell her.

7

I let myself into the apartment that evening, not sure if I'm relieved or disappointed that I didn't run into my new neighbour. Hopefully, he's forgotten all about the coffee. I wouldn't have to remind him that he has a wife.

I can sense Farida isn't at home. She gets tired of staying home all day when she's between commissions and sometimes goes to the nearby park to observe people, or to a cafe, where she ends up drinking so much coffee that she stays awake till 3 a.m. Inevitably, she keeps me awake as well on such occasions, making me watch TV shows with her.

I take a shower, scrounge around for something to munch on and settle down in front of the TV in my comfy jammies, prepared to vegetate. But it's not meant to be. The door opens and Farida enters, her face all flushed and excited.

'Well, hello there. You don't look like you're dressed for a coffee date,' she says.

'Huh?' I respond.

My hand pauses in the middle of shoving chips into my mouth. To my horror, she steps aside and there he is, our new neighbour, smiling sheepishly at me. What is she doing? She's invited him home? I want to run back to my room and shout 'Aaaaaah' like Macaulay Culkin in *Home Alone*. But I just sit there, almost like I've been petrified.

'Hi. I'm sorry, I just got back from the office and was wondering how to approach you, especially since I realized I don't even know your name,' he says.

I still don't know what to say.

'Why don't you sit down for a bit, Ajay,' Farida says, smiling at him and pointing to the single-seater sofa adjacent to where I'm sitting. He looks at me uncertainly and then sits down.

'We could do this some other time if you're . . .' he trails off because Farida has just grabbed my arm and yanked me to my feet.

'No, no, she'll be ready in five minutes,' she says, hustling me to my bedroom.

'What are you doing?' I hiss at her the moment we enter my room.

'Dude, he's not married. Okay, well, he was, but his wife died some years ago. So he's totally available and from what I can see, he's interested in you. Why would you not want to see where this goes?' she asks.

I digest this news in silence. But I'm still not sure I want to go out with him for coffee. I shake my head and make a pleading face to Farida.

'Please don't make me do this. I don't want to go out with him,' I whisper.

'But why? I thought you liked him!' she whispers back in surprise.

'How did you meet him? Also how did you know it was him?' I ask her instead.

She rolls her eyes, looking exasperated.

'I was climbing up the stairs when I saw him heading towards our apartment. He then seemed to change his mind and go back to his. He again turned around, making a move to come here. Obviously, he's confused too. I stopped him and asked if he was our new neighbour.'

Oh. 'Then? When did he tell you about his wife and everything?'

'First off, how could you not tell me about this coffee date?' she asks, glaring, her hands on her hips. I open my mouth to remind her about not having a phone but she shuts me down. 'Don't give me the no phone excuse. Facebook messenger could have done. Anyway, he got talking to me; asked me if he'd overstepped somehow by asking you out for coffee.'

'And?'

'Do we need to do this now? Poor guy is waiting for you outside,' she says.

'Yes, we need to do this now,' I tell her, making a face, although I'm already mentally deciding what to wear.

'So I snapped at him for making moves on you even though he's a married man,' she says. My mouth becomes an 'O'.

'Yeah, he looked rather bewildered but then went on to explain that his wife passed away a few years ago and he's not even sure he wants to go out with other women but he liked talking to you,' she ends softly.

Oh. From what I saw of him, I liked talking to him quite a bit too.

'Okay,' I sigh and then push her outside. 'Tell him I'll be there in five minutes.'

Looking relieved, Farida leaves the room and I turn to my wardrobe, finding my quiet midweek evening thrown out of gear all of a sudden because of an impromptu date with the interesting man next door.

8

I'm feeling awkward and nervous. I smile at him as I step out in my jeans and top which I quickly picked out of my wardrobe because I didn't want to deliberate too long on what to wear. He smiles back at me as we leave the apartment.

I glance at Farida on my way out and she grins while I roll my eyes. This could turn out to be a huge mistake since he lives here and I will inevitably bump into him every now and then.

'I'm sorry I gave you the wrong impression,' he says, looking sheepish. He heads towards the stairs while I walk towards the lift.

'Err . . .' I hate taking stairs but I reluctantly make my way towards him but he walks towards me, opting to take the lift.

'You're a stairs person,' I state because I have nothing to say and I don't want to stare at him too much. It's ridiculous how all these months, even years, I have had nothing going for me and suddenly there's this strapping, good-looking man who literally lives next door and wants to take me out for coffee.

'Out of habit,' he explains as he opens the gate and we step in. 'I take it you're a lift person.'

'Just lazy,' I mutter. 'How come you took the lift yesterday then?'

He actually blushes. 'I . . . I don't know. I wasn't sure why you were following me around. Thought it was the easiest way to get rid of you.'

I'm mortified but he quickly covers up. 'No, I didn't mean it that way. I just . . . I just didn't know what to think. Then you said you lived here and I felt it was serendipitous, meeting you like that.' I don't know how to respond to that so I merely nod.

'I'm sorry. I should have explained this morning about . . . not . . . not . . .' he trails away, looking slightly pained. I realize it's probably still difficult for him to talk about his wife.

'It's okay,' I tell him lamely. 'I'm sorry about your wife.'

The lift creaks to a stop and we get out in silence. 'Where's your daughter?' I ask. Do the two of them live alone? I have so many questions but I'm not sure I can ask them yet.

'My wife's parents live in Bangalore. I was in Pune for a couple of years because my family is there and they took care of Anya while I worked,' he says as we walk towards the gate of the apartment complex.

'Then I was transferred to Bangalore and I thought maybe it would be nice for Anya to be with her mother's family too,' he says.

'So she's with them now?' I ask.

'No, my mother-in-law had come over to help set us up and she's leaving today, so she took Anya out for a bit,' he explains.

I want to ask him where she was in the morning when he was locking up but I don't want to seem too nosy, so I stay quiet.

We walk the tree-lined avenue in silence. There's Costa Coffee on the main road and I realize we're headed there.

'I still don't know your name,' he says as he opens the glass-fronted door.

'Priya. Priya Kumar.'

We order our coffees and sit down at one of the empty tables.

It's weird because we still don't know what to say to each other. After another minute or two of what seems like interminable silence, Ajay speaks.

'Priya, I'll be honest. Thinking back to this morning, I'm actually wincing at the way I behaved and tricked you into coming out for coffee with me,' he says, looking suitably abashed.

'Well, I *was* annoyed. I thought you were hitting on me, despite being married.' He looks chastened and looks down at the table and shrugs.

'I mean, I feel like such an idiot. I spoke to you about Anya, so you knew I was probably married. I don't know why I didn't realize the impression it would have made on you because you didn't know . . . about my wife,' he says.

He looks so adorable as he says this, with his hair sticking out at an angle above his ear, making him look a little goofy, that I want to let him off the hook immediately.

'Listen, it's okay. Let's call it a miscommunication,' I tell him. He looks up, meets my gaze and exhales loudly.

'I've been out of the dating scene for a very long time. After my wife died, I wasn't interested in meeting anyone else. Anya came first for me, and she still does. Sometimes I look around me and feel the world has changed way more than I can handle.'

I nod sagely. 'It happens. I uninstalled Tinder from my phone because I couldn't really find what I was looking for.'

'Tinder is that hook-up app?' he asks, making a face.

'Are you judging me?'

'No,' he shakes his head and I grin.

Our coffees arrive and I watch him tear open a sugar sachet and mix it in.

'I feel like we started off on the wrong foot,' he says as he stirs his coffee.

I watch him take a sip, at the way his eyes sort of crinkle, and I shake my head. Yep. He's totally off the hook.

'I don't think so,' I tell him and am rewarded with another smile.

9

'Why won't you tell me what happened after that?' Farida asks me later that night. I put my bowl down. It's late and I have to sleep. I walked in on Farida throwing a few things together for a stir-fry noodle dinner and when it was ready, both of us took our bowls out to the living room. Farida had lavishly added roasted peanuts to the noodles and it was all sorts of crunchy yumminess.

'This was great. I'm actually glad Parvati akka didn't come today. I think I want some more,' I tell her and get up to refill my bowl.

'You're not changing the topic so easily! What happened?' she calls out. 'Why aren't you telling me?'

'Because nothing happened. We talked a bit and came back. That's all,' I insist as I walk back into the living room. We have a dining table but we rarely use it. It seems so formal and functional. The living room is our favourite spot in the house. It's done up very simply. There's hardly any décor, barring some of Farida's paintings that hang on the walls, but you get the sense of a well-used and warm space. I curl back into my seat and eat some more, thinking about the evening with Ajay.

It's the truth. Something changed when he looked up and smiled at me. Maybe he realized I was as interested in him as he was in me. But, as though through an unspoken agreement, we decided not to discuss it further.

Farida rolls her eyes. 'Come on! I literally set this up for you,' she says.

'You did not!' I counter, throwing a cushion at her which she deftly catches even though she has a bowl in one hand. She tucks it behind her and looks at me primly.

'Well, you'd have spent the evening eating chips if it weren't for me,' she says, making a face. She leans forward and picks up the remote to switch off the TV. The sudden silence is rather unnerving until sounds from outside stream in slowly.

'He spoke about his daughter mostly,' I say finally, hoping that will get her off my back.

'Is that . . . like a problem for you? That he has a daughter?' she asks, leaning forward in her seat.

'I don't know. It's too soon to say anything.' I brush her off. I'd like to meet Anya before forming an impression.

Anyway, it had been a good end to a somewhat rubbish day. I remember how the day began with Mini's breakdown, Namrata asking if I have space for one more person and Vinay looking out of sorts. I tell Farida everything since she knows my colleagues as intimately as if she worked with them herself.

'Poor thing,' she says finally, leaning back and placing her bowl on the coffee table before her. She stretches luxuriously.

'Who?' I ask, curious.

'All of them. I meant poor things,' she amends. 'So much hassle and heartbreak in life. There are times when I'm glad that our lives aren't like that any more.'

'What are you saying? Did you forget that Reshma Phuppu exists? And that we have to get your house back from her clutches?' I ask her incredulously.

'Okay, all of us are poor things then. You're the only one with a perfect no-nonsense life,' she snaps at me. She always gets this wound up when we talk of Reshma Phuppu.

'If only that were true,' I tell her, making a face.

* * *

The morning greets me with the delicious smells of something baking. Farida, apart from being an artist and photographer, is also a fantastic cook. She's probably baking up a storm to make up for the way she behaved with me last night, I think as I head off to shower.

I get dressed and come out of my room with the towel still wrapped around my head and stop in shock. Ajay is sitting at the table, talking to Farida.

At 7.30 a.m. Seriously, doesn't he have any boundaries?

'Look what Ajay got for us,' Farida says, raising one eyebrow at me suggestively. Thankfully, Ajay is not looking at her but at me.

'What?' I ask, although I want to hurriedly run back to my room, remove the towel and come back looking more presentable.

'Cheesy pull-apart bread,' she announces. 'He wanted to leave it and go but I invited him in for tea.'

'Nice,' I murmur, not sure if I should join them at the table or go back to my room.

'I have to leave in five minutes. Have to get Anya ready for school,' he explains, although he smiles at me invitingly. I smile back and nod and finally join them at the table.

'There's tea for me?' I ask. Farida nods and gets up.

'You bake?' I direct the question at him. He nods, a little sheepishly.

'I took a break after Kirti . . . passed away. I was on the verge of a breakdown. Having Anya meant I was responsible for her and yet there were times I needed to get away from it all. I just enrolled in whatever classes I could find, which didn't take me away from Anya for too long. Baking was one of the skills that stuck,' he says.

I'm speechless and I think it shows.

'Priya, are you all right?' he asks, looking worried.

I employ the quintessential non-committal Indian shake of the head, making it absolutely unclear whether I'm saying yes or no.

'Nothing, I'm fine,' I tell him although I am anything but fine. It's just that enrolling in random classes is sort of my thing too. In the weeks following my pottery class, everyone got misshapen pen stands as gifts. And I wasn't very successful with baking either because Farida swore her molar cracked under the strain of trying to bite into the brownie I'd baked. That hadn't deterred me. I continued with these classes during my weekends, trying to fill some sort of empty space inside until I gave up eventually.

'Here's your tea,' Farida says placing my mug of aromatic ginger tea on the table.

'This bread is perfectly warm to eat now. Have some,' she offers me.

I look at the foil container and then at Ajay who is looking at me, still puzzled. I pull the container towards me and break off a piece of pillowy soft bread and nibble. My hunger is like a beast that has awoken in my stomach and it takes all my control not to eat the entire loaf like a starved person in front of Ajay. Give me my carbs in the morning and I'll die a happy person.

Ajay looks taken aback. Shit, I hadn't realized I'd said that out loud.

'Don't mind her. She's mad about carbs,' Farida waves me off.

He nods silently and stands up quickly. I sense that something is off. His expression seems guarded and his mind is somewhere else.

'Thanks for the tea, Farida,' he says. Then, turning to me, he nods. 'See you around.'

He leaves and Farida looks at me, shaking her head. 'What was that all about?'

'Beats me,' I say, stuffing my face with more cheesy bread.

10

It's apparently the week of break-ups at the office. Vinay and Radhika have split up too. I walk into a buzzing office, where heads are converged together and much speculation is taking place over the reasons for the break-up. I glance at Mini's desk and see that she hasn't come in yet.

Namrata walks in, oblivious to all the buzz around her. I wonder what she'd do if she knew her crush was single again. Not much. She's scared of her own reflection half the time. Her constant uncertainty and lack of confidence shows in the way she dresses too. Today she's wearing a mud-coloured tent-shaped salwar kameez which is easily a decade old.

Amrita and Ayaz are back to bullying her, making her do the grunt work while they fiddle around on Facebook, ostensibly working on social media posts while she writes the longer blog posts. I walk in on them an hour later after several mind-numbing meetings—one with the SEO team, one with Arvind Kanakadasa, the CEO of Citron and my boss, who wants to be apprised of our progress every week, and one with the HR manager to inform them that Ayaz and Amrita would soon be leaving. I look at their smug faces and feel pleased that I'll be seeing the last of them at the end of this month.

'Have you guys done *any* work at all?' I ask them as I sit down and stretch my neck to ease out the kinks.

'Sure. We posted those updates that you wanted us to put up,' Ayaz says, his bored voice perfectly matching his demeanour. His arms are crossed above his head and he is swivelling around in his chair.

'What about the blog post I asked you to do?' I question him sharply.

'Namrata is on it,' he says and grins at Amrita who's intently reading a BuzzFeed listicle—'How to know you're working for a Bitch Boss'.

It's my mistake entirely. When they joined, I should have been more aloof and boss-like, but this inane need I have to be liked by everyone will prove to be my undoing. I became all pally with them, taking them out to lunch and even to nearby pubs a couple of times after work. Technically we're in the same decade, but we could have been generations apart. Amrita and Ayaz are both twenty-two, but they have no work ethic whatsoever.

Right. I've got to stop using words like work ethic, which is how thirty-somethings probably talk.

'I heard Radhika was crying in the ladies' room, and then she took the day off and went back home. What is this office, ya? Can I also take a day off if I say I broke up with my boyfriend?' Amrita asks, looking at Namrata's face for a reaction.

Unfortunately, Namrata has no clue she's being played and her expression says it all. There's shock and disbelief written all over her face. Obviously, the grapevine hasn't reached her yet. Before any other expression flits across her face, giving reason to these two to guffaw at her, I get up and ask her to come with me.

'Hey, boss lady,' Amrita calls out as we leave. 'How about giving her a makeover while you're at it? Maybe Vinay will notice her then?'

I hustle Namrata out of our bay, but unfortunately she has heard Amrita's words and the tittering that followed.

'What was she saying?' she asks, as I look for a place where we can talk in private.

'Terrace,' I tell her, and she looks at me uncomprehendingly.

We take the lift to the fourth-floor terrace, where the sun is beating down rather magnificently. There's no one there and I lead her towards the parapet, where we stand silently for a while, watching the busy traffic below.

I take a deep breath. 'How are things at home?' I ask her because now that I have brought her upstairs, I don't know what to say.

'The same,' she says, looking at the traffic.

'Why don't you come home with me today?' I ask her and her face lights up.

'My room-mate, Farida, would love to meet you,' I add. She nods, looking quite happy. I feel bad for not having extended this invitation to her before.

'I have to be back home latest by 8 p.m.,' she says.

'Sure. I'll drop you off if you want,' I tell her, mentally groaning at all the scooter riding my poor back will have to endure.

'No, it's okay. I can take an auto,' she says shyly. I shake my head, remembering her money situation.

'No problem. I'll drop you home. Next time you can visit us on your own,' I tell her.

'Is that an open invitation?'

I turn around in surprise. Mini is walking towards us slowly, a cigarette in her hand. She strolls over to stand beside us, looking down at the traffic, taking a drag of her cigarette every now and then.

She offers it to me but I shake my head. I haven't smoked in ages and I don't want to take it up again. Then, to my amusement and Namrata's mortification, she offers it to her. Namrata literally shrinks away from her.

'Relax. I won't eat you,' she drawls. I look at Mini, at how much she's changed in just a day. Without her make-up, she looks really young and her eyes look denuded without the eyeliner to accentuate them. There are deep shadows under her eyes and the look in them is blank and far off.

'I thought you were on leave today,' I tell her. She shrugs and exhales loudly.

'No need for leave. Have a shitload of work to finish before this quarter. Then I'm done,' she says.

'Meaning?' I'm curious. Mini is always part of the crucial projects at Citron because of her kick-ass coding skills. Whenever a project is about to wind down, they always move her to another that's about to start. I've overheard enough software engineers bitch about how much Citron depends on her to get them out of trouble with projects and how they don't give others the same chance.

'Quitting this sinkhole of a place, dude. I've saved a bit of money and my dad has promised to give me some. Will take a sabbatical and write that novel I've been meaning to write all along,' she says.

I'm surprised. 'Wow. That's cool,' I tell her. I wish I had some sort of well-defined ambition like her. Or talent for that matter.

She shrugs. I glance at Namrata, who is looking at Mini with fascination.

'Are you . . . are you prepared to write a novel?' she asks.

'Yeah. I took a course on creative writing a few months ago,' she says, looking bitter all of a sudden.

'Wasn't good?' I ask, confused.

'It was good. Very good. My ex-boyfriend . . .' her voice wavers a little before she continues. 'Akash was one of my teachers,' she says, turning away from us, continuing to smoke.

11

Later that evening, I call Farida from the office phone to tell her that a couple of colleagues are coming home with me. I sigh when there's no reply. I would have messaged her on WhatsApp if I had my phone, although there's no saying when she would have seen that. She's most likely out and her phone is at the bottom of her bag, nestled in the detritus of a lifetime.

I'm beginning to regret this impromptu invitation because we don't have anything by way of snacks at home. But I can't do anything about it. Also, Namrata is finally showing some signs of life. I briefly wonder just how bad the situation at home must be for her to be excited over something as small as coming over to my house.

Mini suggests that I leave my scooter in the office parking lot because we can all go in her car. I'm tempted at the thought of not having to navigate the fume-filled traffic but then I remember that I promised to drop Namrata off. Mini says she can do that and so I agree.

Mini drives a black Volkswagen, and I envy the grace with which she eases into the traffic. I'm awful at driving a car. I get stiff and anxious and I feel like I can't see everything that's happening around me. If I had to navigate in this traffic, I'd be a mess. Mini, however, cusses her way through. From my front seat, I glance back at Namrata who is looking out of the window, trying to pretend that she didn't hear Mini just call the auto driver, who cut across us, a 'motherfucker'.

Mini seems to be in her element behind the wheel but she's the kind of person who does everything with single-minded precision, like she was born to do it.

We soon reach my home and Mini parks outside the apartment complex because there's no visitors' parking. We get out and start walking towards my building when a familiar figure joins us and I realize my heart is racing. It's become my go-to reaction to him now.

Ajay, however, is not alone. I finally get to see his little girl, Anya. I was beginning to wonder if she even existed. She's holding a ball in one hand and a half-eaten ice cream cone in the other. Her knees are lightly scraped and there are dried tear tracks on her face.

'Hello! You must be Anya,' I say and look up at Ajay and smile. He smiles back rather uncertainly.

Anya blinks and nods but doesn't say anything. I have zero experience dealing with kids this closely so I don't know what to say. I realize Mini and Namrata are still with me, and I awkwardly introduce them to Ajay as we walk into the foyer.

Ajay smiles at them and nods and then heads towards the stairs, but Anya tugs at his hand, so he resignedly turns towards the lift. We all wait for the lift as it grinds its way down to the ground floor.

Inside the lift, we're all crammed in together. I find it a little hard to breathe. It could be because Ajay is standing right next to me and since there's no space, I'm nearly plastered to his side.

I turn my head and so does he. It's a quiet moment, but one that stretches between us. I'm aware that we're not alone but we might as well have been. I feel like I want to talk to him. I want to continue the conversation we were having over coffee. I want to know why his face closed up this morning when I was eating the bread he'd baked for me. But now is not the time; words are not needed for this back and forth that's taking place between us. He smiles just the slightest bit, and I feel that familiar swooping sensation in my stomach when his hand reaches for mine and squeezes it. I try not to show my surprise and instead smile at him tentatively.

The lift stops at our floor then, snapping us out of the moment. Mini pulls open the gate and one by one everyone steps out. I can breathe again. Whew. Ajay pauses while unlocking his door and looks up just as Farida opens ours. Mini and Namrata walk in and I follow them, turning around to look at Ajay who is still looking at me.

12

'You wear strange clothes,' Mini says, looking at Farida, who only narrows her eyes, although she does glance down at what she's wearing—a bright-blue kurta with large splashes of colour, paired with a startling pair of orange palazzo pants. I may have forgotten to mention that Farida likes to dress like a colourful tropical bird. To be fair, all that colour accentuates her fairness. This aspect of her wackiness is one of the traits she inherited from her rather offbeat parents, apart from her artistic talent, of course.

Mr and Mrs Khalil were a memorable couple. It would be hard to find anyone like them even today. Farida's father was an astute businessman who loved to indulge in the fine arts. His study was always full of half-finished canvases; half-finished because he lost interest quickly. Farida often said to me in school that her father liked to be 'artistic' but her mother was the real artist, a sentiment that her father had repeated often enough for it to be parroted by a ten-year-old.

It was true, however. Farida's mother was a talented artist whose paintings were on display in most galleries. She was sophisticated, urban and yet very odd. Farida hated parent–teacher meetings in school because *everyone* would stare at her parents. They wouldn't really wear absurd clothes but they were definitely not anything my mother would have in her wardrobe, especially the colour choices. My mom would shudder a little on seeing them.

'I get a headache just looking at them,' Mom would say sometimes.

At the moment, Farida is checking out Mini with the same expression my mother used to have on her face all those years ago.

'You must be Mini,' she says finally, 'although I don't see why Priya kept calling you the goth chick.'

Mini and Farida size each other up for a microsecond. Then Mini plonks down on the sofa and Farida rolls her eyes at her as she goes into the kitchen. Namrata, always the wallflower, looks on, intimidated. I gently lead her to a sofa.

'Feel free to use the restroom. I'll be back in a minute,' I tell them, going into my room to freshen up. When I come out a little later, Mini is staring down a bowl of nachos while Namrata is holding on to a glass of juice like her life depends on it. Farida is sitting on the single sofa, looking into the distance. Not how I'd imagined my evening. If I have to miss out on talking to Ajay, I might as well make sure the evening is worth it.

'Why is everyone so glum?' I ask as I sit down on the sofa next to Mini who edges away to give me space. She shrugs.

'I don't know man. I just came . . . because . . .' she trails off. She obviously wants to share her heartbreak, but we don't know her well enough so she's not sure how much she can reveal.

'You can tell us about it, Mini,' I say, aiming for a gentle tone but she looks at me and scowls.

'So you can tell everyone in the office? Especially those two fool interns you have working with you?' she snaps. Farida sits up straight and pins her with a glare.

'Speak for yourself. Priya doesn't go around telling everyone's stories to the world,' she defends me.

'Oh really?' Mini asks, not one to back down from a fight. 'Hasn't she told you everything about me? And I'm sure you know all the details about this one's life too.'

Farida's face colours slightly but she continues. 'So? I don't work with you guys. She can come back and talk to me. How does it matter anyway? Don't you talk about stuff that happens in the office to anyone? Your parents?'

'Do I look like I'm twelve?' Mini asks, sitting up. 'Do you tell *your* parents everything?'

'I would if they were alive!' Farida snaps and gets up from her seat. Namrata is looking at this crazy interaction, scared. I'm beyond shocked. I'd never expected this when I invited Mini and Namrata over. For some reason, I thought Mini and Farida would get along well.

Mini's nostrils flare a little. 'Well, my parents are divorced. My mother lives in Mumbai with her new husband and my father is roaming around the world, picking up girls who are easily ten years younger than me.'

'Your father likes . . . very young girls?' I ask hesitatingly.

Mini looks at me swiftly. 'What?' she asks, her voice sounding rather savage.

'I meant . . . you must be how old . . . twenty-three? Twenty-four?' I ask, trying hard not to back down from her angry glare. This is my house after all.

'I'm turning thirty this year,' she snaps at me.

'What? So am I! And Farida too!' I tell her with a smile that slides off my face when I see her glaring at Farida.

'So am I,' Namrata pipes in softly. I'm amazed she has the courage to speak at all.

'Mini, I have to say, no one would believe you if you told them you were thirty. You look nothing like it,' I tell her warmly, hoping this will put her in a better mood.

'Why? How am I supposed to look? Like you? Trying so very hard to fit in with your interns or like her—one look at her clothes and you'll wish you were colour-blind—or her,' gesturing towards Namrata, 'forever wearing sacks to work?' Mini asks.

'Oh my god. Tell her to leave!' Farida says and stomps away to her bedroom. I don't blame her.

'Who wants to even stay here?' Mini growls, standing up. 'You want to come?' she turns to Namrata, who freezes, looking frightened. Mini glares at her for a few moments and then, without any warning, collapses on to the sofa and bursts into tears.

Namrata and I look at each other, not sure how to react. Farida looks out from her bedroom, unable to contain her curiosity. I nod at her to come back outside and, making a face, she does.

Mini continues crying, wiping the streaming tears with the back of her hands, until I pat her back awkwardly. That only makes her cry louder. I look at Farida, alarmed. She seems surprised and scared too. Namrata leans forward and pats Mini's knee.

None of us know what to say. The crying finally stops and she sniffles, taking deep shuddering breaths.

'I'm sorry. I'm sorry for being such a bitch. I just . . . I just don't know what comes over me sometimes,' she hiccups the words. Farida doesn't look too convinced, but she seems to relent.

'Like I said, you can tell us all about it,' I repeat, rather hesitantly. Wiping her eyes, she looks up.

She then tells us everything.

13

'Wow,' I mutter, after nearly an hour.

Mini puts her head back on the sofa, looking exhausted. She shuts her eyes.

'I thought I'd feel better after telling you guys everything, but I still feel shitty,' she says.

'I don't know. Maybe that's just the way you are,' Farida offers. Mini's eyes fly open and she glowers at her. Outside, it's dark.

The coffee table is littered with empty takeaway containers—food we ordered as we listened to Mini relate her grand love story. To be honest, she is a fantastic narrator. It almost felt like we could see her and this guy Akash together. Meeting for the first time in his class, Mini with her scepticism and him with his unending charm, winning her over. It was like a film.

'Did it ever occur to you that he may not have had any plans to leave his wife?' Farida asks the question that has been plaguing me. Namrata looks too scandalized by the entire story to suggest or ask anything.

Mini shakes her head. 'No, I wouldn't have fallen for someone like that. This was genuine. He was very sure that they were getting divorced the moment she came back from the US,' she says.

Despite being worldly-wise and weary, I'm quite sure Mini was naive when it came to this man.

'But obviously he dumped you when she came back,' Farida says.

'Who said she came back? She didn't,' Mini counters hotly.

'If you go to his house, I'm sure you will find him back with her,' Farida continues. 'Why haven't you gone to his house to confront him yet?'

Mini's face turns a little red. 'I don't know where he lives,' she mumbles. Farida wisely chooses to keep silent.

Mini seems to have had enough of sharing her feelings. She stands up and says gruffly, 'I guess I should head home then.' Namrata looks at the time and almost yelps.

'It's 8.30 p.m.!' she says getting up. 'I've never been this late!'

'Relax. It's just 8.30,' Farida tells her. Namrata shakes her head wildly.

'No! I . . . I . . .' she looks at me for help.

'You guys could maybe crash here,' I suggest. Namrata's eyes grow big and Farida turns to glare at me.

'I mean, it could be something of an impromptu girls' night in. We can all talk a bit,' I offer. No one seems interested. Farida looks like she wants to murder me. This is just my way of getting back at her for inviting Ajay home this morning, so I smile at her sweetly.

Namrata shakes her head vigorously. 'No! I can't! My brother will . . .'

'Eat you?' Mini offers unhelpfully. Namrata's eyes fill up with tears and I feel terrible. I know about her situation. The others don't.

'You don't understand . . . I . . .' she starts gathering her things together. I can sense her unhappiness and walk up to her.

'Hey, what's the worst that can happen if you stay back here?' I ask softly. She just continues shaking her head resolutely.

'Call up your folks and tell them you're running late,' Farida suggests but she shakes her head violently.

'Okay fine. I'll drop her home,' Mini concedes, getting up. 'Thanks for the food.'

Farida and I watch them leave. Namrata's face is small with worry and I feel a pang of anxiety for her. I can't imagine someone else having such control over my life. They get into the lift and I wave at them before going back inside.

'Your new phone came, by the way,' Farida says. Thank god! I was beginning to go crazy. 'How could you just invite them to crash here?'

I turn to her as we lock the door to the apartment. She puts her hand up. 'I know this is your place and you can invite anyone to stay here, but that girl . . .' she trails off. She means Mini.

'I know, I was just thinking aloud. It would have been nice. That's all,' I shrug.

'Nice?' Farida fumes, shaking her head.

'Whatever. Just give me my phone,' I tell her as she fetches it. I open the packaging like an excited child and put in my SIM card, which had thankfully escaped unscathed from the rasam attack. As usual, Farida takes the phone away from me. She brings it back minutes later and hands it over.

'Done?' I ask in surprise.

'No, you've got a message.'

'Who?' I ask, taking it from her in surprise.

'Um, guess?' she says with a grin. Shit. My mom, of course.

I unlock the screen and my stomach fills with dread when I read her message. Mom is coming to Bangalore tomorrow!

14

'Things are much better than they were before I came to live with you. So relax,' Farida insists as I go on a cleaning spree later that night.

'You think? I still need to get rid of the alcohol,' I mutter.

'You're almost thirty. You think your mom will be shocked to know that you drink?' she asks.

'You know my mom. Why would you even ask me such a question?' I snap back. To my mom, I'll always be a single-digit age, no matter how old I get. Unless, of course, she wants to remind me that it's time I got married.

'Relax. There's nothing much here that needs that type of cleaning. It's not like we're twenty and she'll find your weed stash and get hysterical,' she tells me with a grin, thinking of the time that had actually happened back when Farida and I were in college. We were staying together in the hostel and mom had come over for an impromptu visit.

'Don't remind me,' I tell her as I wonder what to do with all the alcohol at home. The idea comes to me instantly.

'Listen, I'll just ask Ajay to keep these at his place till Mom goes back.' Farida shakes her head, a sly smile on her face.

'I swear Aunty won't mind if she sees all this stuff here. You can't keep hiding your real life from her. But, by all means, go to Ajay and dump it all there.'

I don't reply as I make my way across the corridor, cradling the bottles in the crook of my arm. Ajay opens the door wearing a faded grey T-shirt and sweats. My eyes instantly travel to his shoulders, noticing how the fabric stretches across them but, before I can admire them too much, I spot the confused expression on his face.

'I'll explain when you let me in,' I tell him, making a face. He pulls the door open and I walk in, looking around. It's like my place, but not as lived-in or nice. More functional. There are some unopened cardboard boxes stacked against the wall; there's an almost unfinished air to the apartment.

'Where's Anya?' I ask, as I place the bottles on his dining table. He looks slightly bemused.

'Asleep. She has school tomorrow,' he says. 'What's going on?'

I take a deep breath and quickly explain the situation to him. The amused smile on his face gives me relief.

'Are you serious?' he asks with a chuckle.

'I swear. She'll flip. I don't know why she has this idea that I'm an innocent and sweet little girl . . .'

'And you keep letting her believe it when you're not innocent or sweet?' he asks softly with a twinkle in his eye. I look up at him and roll my eyes.

'It's easier. I feel better when she's at ease, you know.' I try to explain.

'Fine. I'll babysit your alcohol while your mom is here,' he says.

I thank him and realize that this is it. I have to go back home now, when all I really want is to talk some more.

As though reading my mind, he asks, 'Want a drink?'

'I'd love one,' I tell him with a smile.

'I'm guessing rum, judging from the bottles you've brought over?' he asks as he walks to the kitchen and opens the topmost cupboard, pulling out a bottle of rum and two glasses.

I smile to indicate he's right. I look around the kitchen and ask the question that's just crossed my mind. 'Do you have someone to cook for you guys?'

He shakes his head. 'No, not yet. If you know of someone, can you please let me know? I cook pretty decently but I can't keep up with Anya's demands on most days,' he admits as he hands me a glass. His hand brushes against mine, and I'm forced to acknowledge the weird tension that's been there between us since the lift. I feel butterflies in my stomach as I am reminded of that unspoken exchange. I realize just how much I want to explore this 'thing' further because being here with Ajay right now excites me more than anything else has recently. I've had my share of flings and a couple of somewhat serious relationships but after the initial excitement, things would become stale and boring and I'd constantly be looking for something more.

A part of me is worried that this will go the same way. What if I don't feel like this around him in a few weeks? But that's something to fret about later. And I won't know unless I've actually given this a shot.

We move to the living room and sit down on one of the sofas. I tell him about Parvati akka who does a decent job of cooking for us during the week; she doesn't come on weekends. He takes her details from me, along with my phone number, looking relieved.

As he saves the numbers, I decide to jump into the matter I've been wanting to discuss since I walked into his apartment.

'What happened this morning, Ajay?' I ask. He looks up at me in surprise, prompting me to explain further.

'I mean, you were fine when you were sitting at the table. Then your expression changed completely. I . . .' I break off, not knowing how to continue.

He sighs loudly and runs his hands through his hair. His hair sticks up again but I focus on his words.

'I'm sorry, I didn't realize how it would appear to you. You just made that comment about carbs and you sounded so much like Kirti that it was just a little uncanny,' he says.

I stay silent but there are multiple thoughts vying for centre stage in my head. I sounded like his wife? Is that why he's attracted to me? No, no, no! That's not going to work. Also, I can't constantly be wondering about saying or doing something that reminds him of his wife.

'What's wrong?' he asks, seeing the expressions flit across my face. He looks anxious and moves slightly closer.

'Do I remind you of your wife?' I ask, even though I don't want to hear his answer. He looks surprised.

'What? No. You're . . . you're very different. In looks, in temperament,' he says.

'What do you mean by temperament?' I ask him, slightly annoyed. We barely know each other, so how can he say that?

'I . . . I feel like you'll be pissed at me no matter what I say,' he says, gesturing with his hands helplessly. 'I mean,

I saw you yesterday at the shop before we met at the cash counter. I . . . I couldn't stop looking at you as you hunted the aisles looking for something. You looked annoyed and tired as you kept muttering under your breath but, at the same time, I couldn't stop noticing how pretty you were.'

I feel my face heat up when I realize that we'd been checking each other out and . . . he thinks I am pretty. But before I can say anything, he goes on.

'Of course, you didn't have a bag and, strangely, I had an extra one. Meeting you there was the highlight of my day, my week, my month . . . my year, possibly. And to realize that you lived in the same building? On the same floor?' He exhales loudly and then covers his eyes with his palms.

'God. I sound like . . . like a fifteen-year-old schoolboy,' he says.

I can't help but be charmed as I peel his hands off his face.

'For the first time, in a very long time, my thoughts didn't stray to my wife and that surprised me as well. But then this morning you said something she would most likely say, and it hit me . . . that you and Kirti would have got along so well,' he says, looking at me intently.

I squirm under his steady gaze. His words make me feel warm and wanted, but it's still weird to talk about his wife.

'I . . . I like you, Ajay, but I feel like you're still confused. Maybe you don't know yet what you want from this . . . thing and from me?'

'I do know what I want,' he blurts out, turning to me. My face colours slightly as he takes my glass and places it on the table.

'I wasn't done,' I tell him, my voice coming out as a croak as he edges closer to me, my stupid body already turning to him. Feelings and sensations crowd me, and my mouth seems to dry up completely.

'Talking or drinking?' he asks, his eyes boring into mine.

Both. But I can't bring myself to speak. We need to really discuss this, I think, as I move in closer towards him. But there's no more talking for the next few minutes.

15

'Give me the deets,' Farida looks up from the TV and demands as I let myself in.

'Oh god, not now,' I tell her as I make my way to my room. Knowing her, she's not going to let this go easily. Sure enough, she switches off the TV and follows me to my room.

'No way. I've been waiting to hear everything,' she accuses, making herself comfortable on my bed.

'Arré. We just talked,' I lie, but the telltale blush on my face gives me away.

'Aha! More than just talked, I see. Tell me!'

'Okay, we kind of acknowledged that there's something between us but . . . I can't explain what's happening yet,' I tell her. I'd tried talking to Ajay about it after we'd made out like two teenagers discovering kissing for the first time. After we'd stopped reluctantly, I told him I couldn't be constantly wary of saying the wrong thing in front of him. He admitted that this, us, would take some getting used to.

He'd been busy picking up the pieces of his life and with Anya around, he had not considered other women at all. It was all new to him. There was also some guilt which I sensed. Guilt of letting go of his wife. Of course, we didn't go into detail about that, but I knew this was something that was going to come up.

'So are the two of you, like, together now?' Farida asks, clapping her hands excitedly.

'Err . . . we don't know yet. He asked me out to dinner tomorrow, but,' I shake my head, 'I told him no because Mom will be here.'

Farida's face falls. 'But Aunty will be so happy if you go out with him!' she says.

'See? Exactly. I don't want her making plans and everything. Not right now. Not until I see how things are with him,' I tell her as I settle into bed.

'Okay . . . but you still haven't dished anything,' she sulks.

'Dude. Please. Let me sleep. I have to go to work tomorrow morning,' I tell her, switching off the lights which she immediately switches on again.

'What. Happened.'

'Aargh! We kissed, okay? That's it,' I tell her, wincing.

'Fine. I'll just ask him the next time we meet,' she says sitting on my bed cross-legged.

'Do that,' I challenge her. 'I'm turning off the light now. I really need to sleep.'

'Priya,' she begins again.

'What?' I ask as I lean across and turn the switch off. The room is blanketed in darkness. I can only make out her shape and, when she gets up, I gasp.

'What?' she asks.

'You're glowing!' I tell her.

'Huh?' She looks down and starts laughing. Her orange palazzos are actually glowing in the dark.

'You didn't know they glowed in the dark?' I ask.

She shakes her head and continues laughing. 'I wonder what Mini would think of them now,' she says as she leaves.

She's at the door when I call out to her. 'I hope Namrata didn't get into too much trouble at home.'

'Poor thing. How can she let other people control her life like that?' she wonders. I can see Farida silhouetted in the light from outside and I shake my head. She's a fine one to talk. She hasn't done anything to shake off that horrid aunt of hers.

One day, we need to talk without her jumping to the conclusion that I'm asking her to leave. She shuts the door on her way out. I dive under the blanket and pull out my phone to find that Ajay has messaged me.

This whole day has made me feel like a teenager again, from the girl talk over food and hiding alcohol from my mom to making out with the hot neighbour next door. Now this.

Is it weird that I feel like I know you so well already? The message from him reads.

It is, I reply. *Because we don't. But I'm open to getting to know you better.*

Me too. A lot better, he replies. I grin.

Isn't it late for you? I ask him. It's only 11.30 p.m. but he has to get Anya ready early in the morning.

Not really. I'm used to it, he types back. Before I can add anything, he changes the subject swiftly.

I'm still trying to figure out what I like best about you, he says. My eyebrows lift in surprise.

Umm . . . Am I supposed to respond to that? I type back.

Actually no. I'll figure it out and tell you, but for that we'll have to meet again soon.

I roll my eyes although I'm still smiling and I deliberate about inviting him home tomorrow. But seriously, with Mom around, it would be overkill. Just as I'm wondering what to tell him, a message from my mother pops up on my screen.

I'm all packed! See you tomorrow!

16

Mom's flight will arrive in the afternoon and by the time she gets home from the airport, it will be almost evening. So, I decide not to take the day off from work. I need to know what happened with Namrata.

I enter the office building cautiously, wondering if it was odd that I didn't bump into Ajay this morning. If we hadn't exchanged all those messages last night, I might have wondered if he was avoiding me. But no, he'd sounded fine last night. Maybe he was wondering why I didn't reply to his message about meeting again but Mom's message threw me off and I put my phone away till I fell asleep.

I pull out my phone and type out a message to him, asking if he's left home yet. Just before I press 'send', I change my mind. Ugh. That would be so girlfriend-y and I'm not sure I'm ready for that label yet.

I dump my phone back into my handbag and the moment I enter the work bay, I spot Namrata. She looks at me, smiles briefly and turns away, continuing to work. Amrita is there too, on her personal Facebook page; she doesn't bother to conceal the fact that she's not working.

'Hi!' I say to no one in particular as I dump my bag on my desk and switch on my system. I settle into work as I check emails and schedule meetings, making a list of what needs to be done for the day and whom to assign it to. When I look up, Amrita is not there and Namrata is staring vacantly into space.

'Where did she go?' I ask. She shrugs. I wheel my chair closer to her.

'All okay at home?'

She turns to me and shakes her head. 'It's okay. I feel stupid at times. It's just . . . it was nice to visit you yesterday and I really like your friend Farida,' she says. 'I'm sorry I left in a hurry. I didn't even thank you both.'

'That's okay,' I reassure her warmly. 'Are you still looking for a place to move into?'

She shakes her head. 'I can't leave my mother. She needs me,' she says.

I ponder over that in silence. Mothers. Can't live with them, can't live without them.

'My mother is coming to stay with me for a while,' I tell her.

'From where?'

'Delhi. She lives there with my younger brother. He's twenty-four and such a brat. He went to university in Delhi and then got a job there, which is when Mom decided to move in with him. I moved to this apartment because it was easier to maintain than the big house we were renting earlier,' I explain.

'How come your mother wanted to live with your brother instead of you?' she asks, sounding genuinely curious.

I smile. It's something my brother still hasn't come to terms with. He was horrified when Mom said she would be staying with him. She even got a job after her retirement as an administrative consultant at a school in Delhi. He'd begged her to reconsider and she agreed to stay with him for a few months in a year and spend the rest of her time visiting her sister in Dehradun, her brother in Mumbai and me. So, he was free of her for almost half the year, but she'd made it clear that Delhi was going to be her home base. Secretly, I think she was tired of Bangalore and wanted a change.

'He's the baby and I'm the adult,' I explain. Namrata still looks puzzled.

'And your father?' she asks.

I momentarily freeze at her question. My father is a sore topic for me. Every relationship has givers and takers, but with my father, it was take, take, take all the time. He never stuck with a job long enough to do it well, so it was up to my mother to make sure there was food for us or even that we got an education. She kept hoping he would change but, every few months, he would come up with reasons why his current job sucked and why he had to quit.

Then he decided that working for someone wasn't for him and decided to start a business. Four failed businesses and several loans later, my mother was still supporting the family and paying off his debt. But then my father wanted more excitement in his life, so he had an affair. That was the last straw for Mom. She'd made her peace with bailing him out financially each time, but this she couldn't forgive. She decided to walk away from the marriage for her own peace of mind and I thought it was the best decision she'd made. But obviously, I don't want to get into any of those details with Namrata now.

'My parents are separated. My father moved out when we were in school.' Ugh, I hope she doesn't probe any more about that loser. Thankfully, she lets it go.

'I still don't understand how your mother can leave you to live alone while . . .' she trails off. Living alone must seem like some sort of unattainable dream for her.

'Never mind how my mother's mind works. How was Mini on the way back?' I ask.

'Oh, she was all right. We didn't talk except for when I gave her directions to my house. She lives in Jayanagar and it's not too far from my place in BTM Layout,' she adds.

Amrita saunters in with a bag of junk food. She had obviously gone shopping at the supermarket nearby. Ayaz follows her with a cup of coffee.

'Where were you?' I ask Amrita. She doesn't reply. Just hefts the shopping bag on to her desk.

'You can't do that during work hours. And why are you late?' I turn to Ayaz who is just switching on his system. He doesn't bother to reply.

'Go back to whatever you were discussing, no,' Amrita says, as she pulls out a bar of chocolate and starts unwrapping it.

Ayaz says something under his breath and Amrita giggles. 'What did you say?' I ask.

'Auntyji, auntyji,' he says in a soft sing-song voice, without even looking at me, as he scrolls through Facebook.

My ears heat up first, an indication of the outburst that's been building up inside me all these days.

'Amrita and Ayaz,' I speak softly. Namrata is looking at me warily. Both Amrita and Ayaz continue whispering to each other.

'There's no need for you to come to work from tomorrow. Your internship is over, effective this evening,' I continue in the same tone. The two of them haven't even heard me.

Bloody hell.

'You're fired,' I tell them loudly. They whip their heads up together and look at me, puzzled.

'You can't fire us!' Amrita responds hotly.

'I can. Maybe you didn't realize it, but the two of you work for me,' I say.

The news doesn't seem to affect Ayaz who goes back to scrolling through Facebook.

'Weren't you supposed to retain one of us at the end of the month? We still have ten days left,' Amrita continues. I shake my head.

'Not any more. I've retained Namrata. You two can go,' I tell her.

Amrita crosses her arms and stands up. So do I.

'Listen. I've been in this industry since you were in pigtails. This is not how you behave with your superiors just because they're nice to you. Don't make a fuss and don't come back tomorrow,' I tell her before she can say something nasty.

'The aunty brigade sticks together,' she taunts as she flounces off in a huff. Ayaz looks at me, not a shred of remorse on his face. Instead, there's disgust. Wow. Just what kind of kids are these? They leave together and it's back to Namrata and me, getting the work done for the day.

17

'Are you guys busy?' Mini pops in a while later. Both Amrita and Ayaz have disappeared. I assume they will come back to pick up their things before they leave. I have to inform the HR manager that I've fired them, and I'm not looking forward to it. I don't know if they're aware that they have to meet him before they leave as part of their exit interview. I wonder how much they'll bitch about me. Not that I care.

'We aren't,' I tell Mini, pushing my chair back and stretching. Namrata has just finished writing a blog post and I have to check it before it goes up. I've been planning to train her on how to conduct the webinar as well. I spot Vinay lounging near the coffee machine on our floor. It's not too far from our work bay and if we lean back in our chairs we can usually see who is at the machine. Namrata, who sits beside me, has an even better view.

I glance at her and note that she is pointedly not looking at him. There's a coffee machine on his floor too, so what is he doing here, now that Radhika and he are no longer together?

Mini notices all of this and, for the first time since I've known her, she seems to take in everything around her, in a marked lack of self-obsession.

She glances at me and I nod lightly. She rolls her eyes and mouths, 'No chance.' I know. Namrata is too much of a wimp, and I mean it in the nicest way possible, to actually do anything about her crush on Vinay.

We talk for a bit and then Namrata heads off to the restroom. Mini is just about to leave when the object of Namrata's daydreams walks towards us. Vinay looks around as though searching for someone.

'Er, hi!' I say to him with a smile. He smiles back but still looks a little lost.

'Isn't there someone else who works here with you?' he asks. Mini and I look at each other, wide-eyed. Has he actually noticed Namrata?

'Why?' I ask. His recent break-up with Radhika has given him an edgy look, making him even more attractive than when he was all happy and bouncy like a puppy. Earlier, you'd want to ruffle his hair at how cute he was. He was all clean-cut wholesomeness, with his bright and friendly smile—like Jim Halpert from *The Office*.

Now, there's a certain wolfish look to him, especially with the longer hair, which I'm sure all the girls would appreciate. He hasn't bothered to shave recently and it only makes him look more attractive. Heck, I might have gone for him too, but he doesn't inspire any feelings in me apart from appreciation for his sexiness. Poor Namrata would have melted into a puddle if she'd been here.

'You mean those interns?' Mini asks suddenly, and I realize he means Amrita. Stupid, stupid me.

'Yes,' his eyes light up and my heart sinks. I'd actually thought he was asking about Namrata.

'What about them?' I ask.

'One of them came up to me a while back. Said the other girl who works with you is in love with me. Has been in love with me for a while apparently. I was a bit taken aback. I don't even remember seeing this other girl,' he says.

Aargh! That bitch Amrita. Wait till she comes back for her things. How could she do this?

'So you came to check her out?' Mini asks crisply.

'Whoa. No. I . . . Err . . .' he fumbles in his usual adorable way, and I decide to send him off before Namrata returns.

'Listen. She's a very sweet girl. It's not like that. She's very awkward and shy and she'd be mortified if she came to know about this conversation. So please, just leave. Be a nice guy and don't come back just to see who she is, okay?' I tell him.

Embarrassed, he turns to leave, and bumps into Namrata who is on her way back from the restroom. Like a touch-me-not plant, Namrata seems to shrink into herself. She turns red in the face and looks like she wishes she were invisible.

'Ouch,' Mini mutters under her breath.

Vinay tries very hard not to look at her as he leaves. Namrata walks towards her system stiffly.

No one talks for a while, and I glare at Amrita's bag, wishing I could shoot lasers with my eyes. Such a mean and childish thing to do. If Namrata ever found out, she'd be mortified.

'Okay, I'm going back to work,' Mini says. Namrata is still red-faced and trying hard to pretend she's working so I don't talk to her.

My phone rings and I pick it up in relief. Until I realize it's my mother.

'Why are you at work when I'm here in your house?' she asks.

18

I step into my apartment to the delicious smell of butter chicken as only Mom makes it. My mouth waters instantly as I look around and see evidence of her being in my house already. The centre table has been aligned perfectly with the sofa, the sofas are equidistant from each other and the house keys are in a bowl on the side table and not carelessly left around. And, of course, those tantalizing smells from the kitchen are proof enough.

'I'm home!' I call out and both Farida and Mom walk out of the kitchen talking.

'Finally!' Mom says as she moves forward to envelop me in a hug. She's wearing an apron over her sari and there's a faint smell of fried onions about her.

'You made butter chicken?' I ask even though I know the answer.

'Of course. I can't imagine you're ever going to learn how to make it,' she says. We sit down for some chit-chat, and Farida avoids talking about her home situation, although Mom is like a dog with a bone and keeps coming back to it.

'This time I thought we'll hire a lawyer and kick them out for good,' she says, referring to Reshma Phuppu and her husband.

'Aunty, it's okay. I'm managing. Unless of course you actually want me to go,' she says jokingly.

'Arré, no no!' Mom says, flustered.

The conversation gets a bit strained after that until Mom starts nagging me about getting married.

'But most of your cousins are married,' she says.

'Good for them,' I tell her huffily.

'Some even have kids!'

'Mom, please. I'll get married when I want to, not because I have to,' I tell her looking at Farida for help.

'But you're turning thirty, no?' Mom says.

'Well, so is Farida,' I retort, because that dimwit is doing nothing to help.

'This conversation is about you,' Farida says, making a face at me for reminding her and my mother.

We continue arguing throughout dinner which doesn't taste half as delicious because I'm exhausted from replying to my mother's queries. By the time I go to my room to sleep, I'm pretty beat. Then I realize she's going to sleep with me while she's here. Great.

She's sorting out stuff in the kitchen so I snuggle under the blankets and pull out my phone. Ajay has messaged, asking how things have been with Mom.

I quickly type out a reply, to which he responds immediately, and we continue chatting. He tells me about Anya, and I tell him about my mother.

You're probably just exaggerating. I'm sure your mom is very charming, he writes.

Don't count on it. I'm sure you'll run into her sooner or later, I reply. We chat a bit more till I fall asleep, feeling a little better.

Morning arrives sooner than I would like. I get dressed for work, glad that it's a Friday, not sure if I should look forward to the weekend (because I'll get to meet Ajay) or dread it (because I'll have to face a fresh set of marriage questions from Mom). I'm just leaving my room when Mom walks in, excited.

'What happened?' I ask her.

'I just bumped into this very nice young man who lives on your floor,' she says.

'Nice young man?' Farida asks from the living room, looking at me slyly.

'Ajay?' I ask, feeling dread curl inside already.

'Yes! Yes!' Mom says.

'What were you doing up so early?' I ask her, hoping to deflect her from Ajay.

'Arré, I can't give up my morning walks just because I'm visiting you! I was leaving when he was going to drop his daughter off to school,' she says. God, my mother is so transparent. I can literally see the wedding invitations dancing around in her eyes.

'And? What did you do?' I ask her warily.

'Nothing. What do you think I would do? I thought it was really sad that his wife is no more and he and his daughter live all alone,' she says.

'You met him for two minutes and you already know about his wife?' I ask incredulously.

Mom ignores my remark. Her interrogation skills are on a par with the CIA.

'I've invited them for dinner tonight, okay? Wear that turquoise-blue salwar kurta I bought the last time I was here. None of this jeans nonsense,' she says, rubbing her palms together, already planning the evening.

'Mom!' I wail. It's one thing for me to chat him up and, you know, probably something more a little later. It's another thing for my mom to interfere.

Farida just keeps grinning.

19

I'm about to leave for work, wondering what I can tell Ajay that will put him at ease about this whole dinner thing, when I notice Farida hunched over her laptop, looking troubled.

'Hey, are you okay?' I ask, sitting across from her at the dining table.

She sighs. 'Aunty is right you know. I should kick those two out. I need to find a lawyer,' she says.

'Look, you can stay here for the rest of your life but that house is rightfully yours and you need to take it back,' I tell her. She nods and, of course, since we've been friends forever, I know that look.

'But that's not why you're so worried,' I state. She looks up.

'I was searching for Irshad,' she admits quietly. I know I'm going to be late for work today. But it can't be helped.

'I thought you'd already looked for him everywhere.'

'I don't know. I just . . . I just don't know what to do,' she says, a faraway look in her eyes.

'Look, umm . . . even if you . . . I mean, how would you know it's him? You guys haven't met in nearly two decades,' I remind her gently.

Farida's face flushes. 'I'll know,' she says stubbornly.

'Why are you looking for him now?' I ask, leaning across and squeezing her hand gently.

'I don't know. I just . . . he and his parents are my only family apart from Reshma Phuppu. I want to find him,' she says. We sit in silence for a while, each thinking of Irshad, a distant maternal cousin who had once briefly visited Farida's family with his parents. We'd both been quite taken with him because he was from London and spoke with a fancy accent. Farida and I were neighbours and classmates then; we were inseparable. With Irshad joining us, the three of us had quickly become very good friends in the short time he was here. Yet, there was a unique bond between him and Farida.

Farida has never really had a proper relationship with anyone because of Irshad. It's dumb, I know, to fall in love with someone when you're only ten and wait for them like this. After Irshad left with his parents, they'd exchanged letters for a couple of years. But then Farida's parents died and Reshma Phuppu swooped in and changed everything. Farida tried writing to him again but Reshma Phuppu made sure the letters never reached him. She tried calling him, only to discover that their ISD calling had been disconnected. I'd asked her to try from my house and we realized that my father had disconnected ours as well. Years later, when we all had mobiles, she'd tried calling the number that she'd memorized as a kid, only to find that his number had been disconnected.

Farida had been heartbroken for the longest time, wondering how he could forget about her so callously. Why hadn't he called her even once? Farida's father had married her mother against his family's wishes and had been estranged from them ever since, which was why Reshma Phuppu's arrival was such a surprise. Farida's mother had been an only child and all her distant relatives, like Irshad's parents, were scattered all over the world. Farida hadn't even known of Irshad's existence until he'd shown up with his family that summer. So there was no way for her to find him through mutual relatives and acquaintances.

Every now and then she searches for him online, on Facebook and LinkedIn, but she has no idea what he does for a living and there are way too many Irshad Ahmeds to narrow it down.

'We'll find him one of these days,' I comfort her. She doesn't seem to hear me as she clicks on yet another Irshad Ahmed on Facebook, trying to see if it is her long-lost cousin.

I end up leaving half an hour later than usual and miss bumping into Ajay as a result. My mind is so clogged with different thoughts, wondering how I can help Farida and find Irshad, that, as I turn towards the office parking lot, I inadvertently slow down and a speeding scooter careens straight into mine, knocking me down.

Momentarily, I'm stunned. I try to get up just as someone lifts the scooter away. Then I realize why people are standing around gawking. My palazzos—borrowed from Farida because I was in the mood—have ridden all the way up to my thigh.

Uff! I dust my palms and straighten my clothes, glaring at the leering onlookers. The few helpful people are being rather sweet. One of them is the office watchman and the other is Vinay. Great.

'I'm fine! I'm fine,' I protest as Vinay helps me up and the watchman wheels my scooter into the office parking lot. I've got a slight scratch on my elbow from where it connected with the road, and my shoulder and knee hurt but I limp my way into the building, refusing any more help.

I should have known then that this wasn't going to be a very good day.

20

The office has imploded with the gossip that Namrata is in love with Vinay. I hear the whispers everywhere I turn. I realize this must have been Amrita's parting shot. I never got to give her a piece of my mind yesterday because she hadn't returned when I left.

Mini looks at me grimly and nods in the direction of the terrace. Surprised and even somewhat thrilled that I'm cool enough to be her friend or even someone she shares things with, I follow her up there.

'It's crazy. Everywhere I go, people are talking about her,' Mini says, shaking her head. 'I mean, normally I don't notice people but this . . . it's become something else.'

'What can we do? It's a wonder she hasn't realized anything yet. But the moment she knows, she would want to quit, and I can't let that happen,' I tell her.

'You know it would be kind of cool if she did manage to snag him after all this drama,' Mini says, looking down at the traffic below.

'You think?' I ask her as my phone buzzes with a message. It's from Ajay.

Dinner at your place tonight? With your mom? She's invited me.

I look up at Mini, momentarily distracted, and then hit upon an idea that's devious but also brilliant.

'Mini, do you want to come to my house for dinner tonight?' I ask her.

'Huh?' she looks taken aback. 'Wha . . .'

'My mom is visiting and she wants me to invite a few friends over,' I explain.

'Okay,' she says slowly. 'I . . . but . . . okay I'll come.'

Great. I type a reply to Ajay.

Nothing like that. I'd invited a few friends for dinner and Mom thought it would be nice to have you and Anya over.

He comes back online, sees the message but doesn't reply. He's probably busy. But it's good I was able to come up with this idea. I don't want him to think that Mom has invited him over with some ulterior motive in mind. He'll be cool if it's dinner with friends. Or so I hope.

'Priya, what about Namrata?' Mini asks. 'I don't know how long we can shield her from all this fucking gossip,' she says as we make our way back downstairs.

'You know what, I'll invite her too,' I tell Mini.

'What? You know the fuss she made that day, right? Dinner will be later than 8 p.m.!' she protests.

I know. Another idea has been forming in my head, one that could really backfire, but instead of ignoring it, I let it snowball into something big.

Mini rushes off while I limp downstairs slowly. I spot Vinay who is lurking around our bay, ostensibly searching for something. Namrata, who is dressed in an off-white and

green salwar kameez, looks a little green herself. She's aware
of the looks she's getting from everyone but is apparently still
unaware of the reason. Thank god for that, I think.

She looks at me in concern as I walk towards her slowly,
wincing. 'What happened? Why are you limping?'

'A scooter knocked me down,' I reply.

'Are you all right?' She looks shocked.

'Yes. Just a couple of scratches and, of course, everyone
on the road saw my thighs. I mean, normally I don't mind if
people see my legs when I'm wearing a short skirt, but it was
different when these palazzos rode all the way up.'

Namrata's eyes widen. 'Oh my. I'd have died if that
happened to me,' she says and pats my hand gently. 'Oh you
poor sweet girl', I think. I look around us; the idea that has
been building in my head is egging me on.

'My mother is visiting and she's having a small dinner
party tonight. Please come. I've asked Mini also. She said
she'll drop you back like the other day,' I tell her.

'I . . . no, my brother . . .' she stutters. It's clear as day that
she's thrilled to have been invited but she's too scared.

'Please? Also, I've been thinking, how about we get you a
haircut?' I ask.

'What? Why?' Her eyes are wide and startled. It's as if the
idea has never occurred to her.

'You keep hiding your face behind your hair. A good
haircut will frame your face properly,' I tell her, hoping I don't
sound too patronizing.

She looks tempted and then seems to remember
something and becomes downcast again. 'I don't think I have
that much money,' she says.

'That's okay. Let's have some fun with my credit card today,' I tell her. She shakes her head wildly.

'I can't!' she protests.

'It's nothing really. Didn't you say you're turning thirty this year? It's my birthday gift to you. Please!' I convince her. Her eyes fill up with tears but she doesn't say anything and returns to her work.

I honestly don't know why I'm doing all this. I think changing her look will give her confidence and the people who have been whispering about her all morning will shut up when they see her in a different light.

Right. Also, pigs will fly. And I'm Aishwarya Rai.

21

Mini looks doubtful when I tell her about the plan to get Namrata a haircut. We're at the reception post lunch, whiling away what's left of the hour. Namrata has excused herself, saying she has to make a call home to tell her family she'll be late.

Mini puts away the day's newspaper 'Why? How will that help her?'

'I don't know.' I'm not sure of my motives but Amrita's words keep playing in my head. 'I feel she'll be more confident,' I add lamely.

'And you think she'll attract Vinay's attention?' Mini asks. 'I mean why would you even decide that for her? You're not some fairy godmother.'

Ugh! Trust Mini to be blunt. 'You're right. But I'm . . . I'm not trying to be a fairy godmother. I just want her to be more comfortable in her own skin. She looks like a deer caught in the headlights most of the time.'

Mini exhales loudly. 'You're weird, you know that? I've been in Citron as long as you but it's strange how we never connected before. Have you always been this meddlesome?'

'Meddlesome?' I ask her, my mouth agape in outrage. 'I'm not—'

'You are too. You say you want to change the way she looks. You're hoping Vinay will look at her. You're a bloody matchmaker. That's what!' Mini says, shaking her head in exasperation.

Aargh! No! That would be my mother, not me. My heart sinks the slightest bit when I realize that maybe she's right. I must have inherited some of my mother's ways.

Mini's still frowning, but then she shrugs and says, 'I didn't mean to be hard on you. Let's hope your plan doesn't backfire.'

'How will it backfire?' I ask her but she's already walking away.

'See you this evening!' she calls out. I'm somewhat glad Mini is my friend now. I feel this whole thing with Namrata and Vinay has taken her mind off her own break-up. She's looking more alive and is back to her goth make-up, which, frankly, I love. But trust her to put her own spin on things and make me feel bad about helping someone out. I decide not to offer wardrobe suggestions to Namrata because that would be even more meddlesome and annoying in Mini's books, and Namrata is too sweet to tell me so to my face.

Send me some pics of her afterwards, okay? Mini texts me as I go back to my desk. Namrata and I would have left early but I was training her for the webinar in one of the conference rooms and it took longer than usual because of all the curious stares that constantly kept coming our way.

When we finally head downstairs I can sense Namrata is a little excited. I'm not sure how well the call to her family went because she looked grim when I got back from the reception.

My knee and shoulder have begun to hurt and I feel a little idiotic for doing this now. But I really do want to help her. I can't believe that she still hasn't cottoned on to the fact that she's the subject of office gossip.

We hop on to my scooter and make our way to the mall but, once there, she has an attack of nerves.

'I don't think I can do this,' she tells me as she stares at the salon door.

'Okay,' I tell her, feeling a little disappointed. 'If you like your hair so much, then let it be.'

'No, it's not that I like my hair. It's just . . . my mother and my brother . . . they will . . .' she trails off.

I shake my head, deciding to try one more time. 'You're almost thirty now,' I tell her, cringing inwardly. How I hate that number. It's just so unwieldy. 'You should be able to decide if you can cut your hair or not.'

I can tell she's still somewhat frightened, but she agrees and we go in. She tells the hairdresser not to make a drastic change while I tell her to cut it and style it so it will highlight her features better.

As the hairdresser sprays her hair with water and starts cutting the edges higher and higher, I can see the transformation take place in front of my eyes. It's like watching a butterfly emerge from its cocoon. And what a butterfly it is!

I look at her amazed as the hairdresser finally steps away. Her hair has been styled in loose waves that fall gently around her face, highlighting its symmetry. She looks at me in the mirror, stunned.

'I . . .' Words fail her, and I place my hand on her shoulder.

'You look amazing,' I tell her and she places her hand on top of mine.

'Thank you. I don't know what to say. Why are you doing this?' she whispers.

My face flushes slightly with guilt as Mini's words come back to me. I think of all the gossip in the office, even though I'm not responsible for it. I just take a picture of her and send it to Mini on WhatsApp. She replies with the goggle-eyed emoji and I grin slightly.

'Let's go,' I tell her. My house is not too far away, but by the time we reach home, my whole body is aching from the fall. Namrata is concerned when she sees the pronounced limp as we take the lift to my floor. Farida opens the door, dressed in black and shocking pink, her hair done up in an artfully messy boho topknot. I let Namrata explain everything as I head to my room for a hot shower, hoping that will ease the pain.

Mom emerges from the kitchen, her brow shiny with sweat, and I quickly escape to my room because she will order a proper inquisition once she hears about my fall, and I want to be ready before Ajay comes.

The hot water stings but also soothes, and I feel refreshed as I step out with the towel wrapped around my body.

'Jeez. You gave me a fright,' I tell Farida who is sitting on my bed, waiting for me, my hand on my chest.

'Drama queen,' she mutters. 'Listen, we have to talk. About your mom's plans for you and Ajay.'

'What?'

I sit down beside her on the bed and she tells me what Mom has been saying all morning. She thinks Ajay is perfect marriage material and the fact that he comes with a daughter is a plus point.

'She got all this from five minutes of conversation with him?' I ask, incensed.

Farida shrugs. 'What can I say? Your mom is a determined woman. By the way, is that really Namrata?'

'Yes, it's her. She looks good, no?' I ask, as I get up and limp my way to the wardrobe.

'Amazing actually. I wouldn't have recognized her. She seemed so mousy when she came home that day. Today she's vibrant and glowing. How did that happen?'

I quickly tell Farida about what's happened in the office and she narrows her eyes when she hears that Mini is also coming for dinner.

'You're telling me now?' she asks.

'Um, sorry. I meant to message you, but I forgot. There's enough food, right?'

Farida's nostrils flare a little as she walks out without bothering to reply. I roll my eyes and then hunt around in my wardrobe for clothes to wear.

I spot the turquoise-blue salwar kameez that Mom wanted me to wear but instead pick a dove-grey sleeveless sheath dress that flows beautifully and falls a little below my knees. I'm not sure if it's a good choice because though it shows off my arms, my elbow is grazed and my shoulder hurts. Nevertheless, I wear it, fix some pearl studs in my ears and do up my face, wincing as the pain radiates from my shoulders. I brush out my hair and leave it loose to add glamour to my look.

I step out feeling pretty good and Namrata looks at me appreciatively and smiles. Mom, who is at the dining table making the salad, glares at me for not having worn what she chose. Farida who has been working with her, nods.

'Do you mind helping a bit?' she asks and Namrata gets up immediately.

'I'll help!' she says. The doorbell rings and there are nervous flutters in my stomach. I know this whole dinner scene is bizarre but I want to look good no matter what.

'I'll get the door,' Namrata says.

Our jaws hit the floor when we see Vinay standing at the door, looking sheepish.

22

Namrata freezes, and I quickly take charge.

'Vinay! Hi,' I tell him, opening the door wider to see Mini standing behind him, grinning wickedly. What has she done? I gently tug at Namrata and pull her to one side, letting Mini and Vinay come in.

'Hi Priya,' Vinay says, looking around uncomfortably. 'I swear I didn't mean to gatecrash your dinner party but I bumped into Mini at the supermarket and she . . .'

'Forced him to join us for dinner,' Mini ends, looking triumphant. Sometimes, all the stereotypes about beautiful but dumb are true, I think savagely. How can she be so dense? Namrata *just* stepped out of her comfort zone. She's not ready to meet Vinay of all people, though he can't seem to take his eyes off her.

I welcome him in with what I hope is a gracious smile. 'Vinay, this is my mother, that's Farida, my friend and flatmate, and you know Namrata, right? She works with me.'

Vinay smiles stiffly at everyone and looks lost, so I lead him to the sofa and tell him to sit. Thankfully Farida steers Namrata towards the dining table where she enlists her help and starts talking to her to make her feel at ease. Mini sits down opposite Vinay and offers to help with dinner. I feel like telling her that her help has been more of a hindrance but I don't because the doorbell rings again.

This time when I open the door it's Ajay with Anya. He's dressed casually in jeans and a shirt and Anya is wearing a cute little crop top with jeans. I flush slightly as he looks at me, flashing a special smile for me before smiling at everyone else and nodding in their direction. He walks in holding a foil-wrapped dish, which he hands to my mother, who beams at him.

'You shouldn't have!' she says, but looks thrilled. I introduce everyone while Anya looks around, already bored.

'Do you want to watch some TV?' I ask, not sure how we're expected to entertain a five-year-old.

She looks at Ajay, who nods almost reluctantly. 'I try not to let her watch too much TV,' he explains when I look at him puzzled. I nod because I don't know what to say. Ajay the parent is different from Ajay the man, and I am only somewhat acquainted with the latter.

I switch on the TV and we settle on a channel that she likes. Ajay walks over to Mom and strikes up a conversation with her. Farida smiles at him politely and, while Vinay is flipping through a magazine, I quickly motion towards Mini and Farida and ask them to come to my room. Namrata who has been helping Mom looks at us in surprise but doesn't say anything. I realize with a pang that she's probably used to being left out.

'*What* were you thinking?' I turn to Mini as soon as we shut the door to my room.

'What? I thought she looked really nice in that picture you sent me. And I swear I didn't deliberately go looking for Vinay. He was there, in the supermarket, hunting for those ready-to-heat-and-eat food thingies and I thought the poor chap would enjoy your mother's food,' Mini says.

'Mini, but . . . it's just . . . she's not ready yet! I thought she'd have the weekend to get used to this whole new look of hers,' I protest. Farida taps her foot impatiently.

'Look, you two fight it out. I'm going back out. Your mom is ready to serve dinner in five minutes,' she says and turns to leave. At the door though, she looks at Mini.

'I always used to think Priya couldn't stop herself from meddling in other people's lives, but you've taken it to a whole new level,' she says, unknowingly echoing Mini's words to me this afternoon. Mini narrows her eyes and crosses her arms defensively.

'Look, so what if he's here? Let's behave like everything is normal, okay? She has to get used to the attention now, thanks to you,' she says.

'Yes, but if things go wrong, I feel like she will want to quit. And I don't want that,' I tell Mini earnestly.

'Why do you care?'

'I do care,' I snap at her and then tell her what I know of Namrata's life. Mini looks slightly abashed at the end of it all.

'Look, I'm sorry I didn't know all this. But it has nothing to do with this. She won't quit. She's just got a major confidence boost thanks to you. She'll handle everything perfectly.'

'Fine. Whatever,' I grumble and we both leave the room. Outside, my mom is setting the table with Namrata's help.

'Here, let me do it. You go and sit down. You're the guest here,' I tell her as I take the plates from her.

'No, no, Priya. Let me help,' she mutters. Sitting down would mean that she would have to face Vinay. The doorbell rings and Farida looks at me suspiciously.

I shrug. I haven't invited anyone else. But Farida, who is closer to the door, opens it and steps back in shock.

A heavyset woman in a shiny silk salwar kameez barrels her way in and grabs Farida's shoulders, shaking her hard. 'You bitch! You bitch! You bitch!' she screams. Everyone looks shocked at the scene that is playing out.

I recover my wits quickly and step forward to push the woman away. It's not easy.

'Reshma Phuppu, get out of my house,' I tell her quietly.

23

Mini steps in, eyes wide as she yanks Reshma Phuppu away from a shocked Farida.

'This girl—this bitch—she tried to seduce my husband,' Reshma Phuppu rants, looking like a madwoman. Her bulky arms jut out from the tight half-sleeves of the kameez, making her look a bit like a formidable wrestler. Her hair, in an untidy bun, is askew and her face is red with the effort of controlling her anger.

Farida turns pale. What devious lies has her husband told her?

'That's a lie,' Farida replies, her voice quivering with emotion.

'Look woman, you can't come here and make a scene like this,' Mini says firmly, pushing Reshma Phuppu, who seems more incensed to see Farida in the middle of a warm family gathering.

'Who are you to tell me what I can and cannot do?' Reshma Phuppu asks, pushing Mini. I can't believe this is happening. I'd expressly told our watchman to never let this woman in and yet here she is, twice in one week. My poor mother looks like she's about to faint. Ajay is frowning, Vinay looks uncomfortable and Namrata's eyes are wide in horror. Anya thankfully hasn't moved from the TV.

'I'm her friend,' Mini says, shoving Reshma Phuppu hard enough so she staggers back.

'Mini, leave her,' Farida says quietly but apparently Reshma Phuppu needs someone like Mini who won't be bullied.

'Get out and don't ever come back,' Mini says, shoving the woman towards the door.

'Not until I take my revenge on this bitch,' Reshma Phuppu screeches and steps forward, fat fingers outstretched as though to pull Farida's hair from the roots. This is insane. The door to our apartment is open and I'm surprised people from the other apartments haven't come to see what the commotion is about.

'Your husband tried to molest me. That's why I moved out of my own house,' Farida says. Apart from Reshma Phuppu's heavy breathing and Dora the Explorer's queries on TV, there's silence in the apartment.

'Nonsense! He told me you were always giving him coy looks and when that didn't work, you tried to seduce him!' Reshma Phuppu shouts.

'Just the thought of your husband is enough to make her vomit,' I intervene. 'Enough to make all of us vomit. I'm calling the police if you don't leave.'

Farida looks like she's really about to vomit and runs to her room. Mini looks at her and then, with renewed energy, pushes Reshma Phuppu out of the door.

She quickly shuts the door, but the woman continues to bang on it and hurl abuses at us.

'Call your building security!' Mini urges me. I dial the number quickly.

Ten minutes later, the guard has firmly escorted her out of the complex. Reshma Phuppu is gone, but it looks like the dinner party is ruined. Mom looks stunned by the turn of events and that's how all of us feel. I go to Farida's room and find her in the bathroom, washing her face.

'Please just go. I don't feel like joining everyone,' she murmurs as she steps out, wiping her face with a towel.

'No way. I'm not letting you stew in self-pity. You're coming with me,' I insist.

'I can't, Priya! Please,' she insists and looks up in surprise at Mini who is standing by the door.

'I kicked her out. There's no way she's coming back. Come out, please,' she tells Farida, whose face turns red. She covers her face and shakes her head.

'I'm so embarrassed,' she whispers, as I hug her. She cries quietly, while Mini steps into the room, followed by Namrata.

'I'm so glad Mini is on our side,' Namrata whispers, surprising us all. Mini snorts and then laughs.

'I mean, the way you pushed her out,' Namrata says with a slight giggle.

'That's the first full sentence you've spoken to me,' Mini announces.

Namrata takes a deep breath. 'I . . . I feel so stupid at times. I keep thinking about how my life is such rubbish and then all this happens and—' she breaks off because Farida is frowning.

'No, I mean . . . I don't pity you, Farida. I just realized that everyone's life is tough,' she stutters.

'Come on, girls. I'm hungry,' Mini says.

The four of us emerge from Farida's room and Mom looks relieved to see us. She probably thought she'd have to send away the other guests. Ajay is trying to make Anya eat and he looks at me with concern. I smile to put him at ease and head over to help Mom serve dinner.

Somehow, after all the drama, the dinner party actually improves. There are no more awkward pauses and everyone talks freely about what happened over the delicious food.

'Mrs Kumar, I haven't had such a good meal in months,' Vinay proclaims from the sofa.

Mom flushes with pleasure. 'You should learn how to cook like our Ajay here,' she says.

Our Ajay? Ajay and I share a look and I shake my head slightly.

'He brought this tandoori paneer shashlik,' Mom says proudly. Ajay looks a little uncomfortable at the praise and turns to Farida.

'I have a couple of good lawyer friends. I can put you in touch with someone.' Farida nods. She's finally accepted that Reshma Phuppu has to go. I don't know why she waited this long.

'You were amazing, the way you stood up to her,' Vinay says to Mini, admiration in his eyes. Mini grins.

'I was always the school bully, so it wasn't difficult to channel that again,' she replies.

It would be too much to expect Namrata to join the conversation, although I'd say she's progressed in leaps and bounds because she's actually eating and smiling now. I look at Anya, who has become quite sleepy. In fact, halfway through our meal, she falls asleep on one of the sofas.

'We have to get going,' Ajay says as he hefts Anya across one shoulder.

'But you're right next door,' Mom protests, giving voice to what I want to say. 'It's a holiday tomorrow. Sit for some time, please? Have dessert at least.'

Ajay looks torn. 'Okay, let me just put her to sleep and I'll come back for dessert,' he promises and turns to leave.

'We have to leave too,' Mini announces. Mom waits a while for Ajay but since it's getting late, she serves the malai kulfi.

After everyone has scraped their bowls clean, Mini stands up and says, 'Thanks for the food, Mrs Kumar.'

As the others echo her sentiment, Namrata looks at the time. It's 10 p.m. Her face pales when she realizes that Vinay will also be joining them for the ride back to her place.

24

I'm actually dying to know what happened or didn't happen on that car ride but, of course, I need to wait a while before I can call Mini and ask her for details. Meanwhile, Mom is cleaning up and Farida and I help her. Ajay didn't come back for dessert and I'm a bit disappointed. I wonder if he felt awkward because of my mother's remarks. I feel tired as these thoughts swirl in my head. I'm glad tomorrow is Saturday and I can sleep in.

'Did Ajay give you the lawyer's number?' I ask Farida, who shakes her head. I look at the clock and decide to call Mini, but she doesn't answer. Disappointed on all counts, I change and get ready for bed when my phone pings. Mom, who has been slaving away for this dinner party all day, is already asleep and snoring gently. It's a message from Ajay.

Sorry, I couldn't get away. Anya woke up and wouldn't let me leave until I'd read her a bedtime story. Then she took too long to fall asleep.

Oh. *That's all right,* I type back.

Any dessert left?

Now? I look at Mom to check if she's sleeping and gingerly get up.

Yes, now.

Feeling a bit like a teenager on a forbidden date, I quickly skip out to the kitchen and open the freezer. Mom has, of course, saved some kulfi for him in a takeaway container. How convenient, I think.

I unlock the main door, lock it behind me and step out into the darkened corridor, my keys and the kulfi in my hand. I look down at myself and wince. I'm wearing a terrible-looking comfortable cotton top with faded pink yoga pants. Yuck. But it's too late to change now and it's not like I'm going there to seduce him.

I'm outside your door, I message him and the door opens almost instantly.

His living room is dark, except for a light in the corner casting a nice, toasty glow. We sit down on the sofa and Ajay takes the container from me eagerly. Err . . . he really did want just the dessert then, I think, bemused.

'Thank you!' he whispers and starts digging into it with a spoon. 'Wow. Yum!'

I nod, not knowing what to say. I look around the living room and see a framed photograph that wasn't there a couple of days ago. I would have noticed it, I'm sure. I walk over to the coffee table and pick it up.

In the photo, Anya is really little. Just about a year old. Ajay is holding her and his other arm is thrown around a woman's shoulders, who I assume is his wife. She's fair, has a small nose and is uncommonly pretty. There's a sense of elegance about her that makes me feel dowdy in comparison, like a Raggedy Ann doll. But what strikes me the most is the expression on her face. She's looking at the two of them with such love in her eyes that I almost step back from the photo. It feels like I'm intruding into a sacred space.

'That was taken just months before she died,' Ajay says, coming to stand behind me. He places his hands on my shoulders and I turn around.

'I'm so sorry,' I mutter, looking down. He sighs audibly.

'Yeah. I could never bring myself to display that photo. It hurt too much. But after I moved here, I don't know . . . it felt safe to take it out,' he says. I frown at his words. Safe?

'How . . . how did she die?' I ask instead.

'Her bus met with an accident on the highway. There were lots of casualties. She was one among them.'

'Oh no! I . . . I can't imagine how it must have been for the two of you,' I tell him, horrified. I really can't imagine losing someone like that.

He nods sombrely. 'It felt like my world had ended,' he says. 'It took me months to be functional again and that was only because of Anya.'

We fall silent for a few moments, me clutching the photo, he lost in his thoughts. 'I'd better get going then,' I say finally. My heart is aching for him and Anya.

He pulls me closer and I look up at him, surprised. Seeing the photograph has completely killed my mood. Ajay's grip on my shoulder tightens slightly and I wince.

'What happened?' he asks, moving his hand away immediately.

I tell him about the fall this morning and he looks concerned.

'Why didn't you go to the doctor? Are you sure you're fine?'

'It's nothing. It was more embarrassing than anything else,' I tell him about those stupid palazzos riding up and he grins.

'There are a number of things I can say about kissing you where it hurts and making it go away but you might find it a bit creepy,' he says, bending his head closer. Despite the initial butterflies in my stomach, the atmosphere of intimacy and the light-heartedness in his voice, I stop him by putting my hand on his chest. He looks up, surprised and confused.

'I'll see you soon,' I tell him and leave.

'You looked great tonight,' he calls out softly as I open the door. I turn around briefly and smile, although I walk back to my door with a heavy heart. My mind is still on his wife's death and how it must have devastated him. It seems as though he's bounced back from it now. But his confession about being able to display his dead wife's photograph because it felt safe niggles away at me.

Back in bed, I pick up my phone and see there are a couple of messages from him.

Thanks for the kulfi.

No problem, I type back, feeling a bit flat emotionally.

Is everything okay?

I don't know, I type out and then erase it. Then I retype it and erase it again. I put the phone on my bedside table without replying to him and fall asleep.

25

Only when I wake up in the morning do I remember to call Mini.

'Man, her family is completely fucked up,' she drawls, her voice even huskier with sleep.

'Why?'

'I thought it was best if I dropped her at the door personally. I got down. Vinay was still in the car. Also, side note, remind me to tell you how he couldn't take his eyes off her,' she says.

'What?'

'Yes, but listen to this first,' she says and goes on to relate the events of the previous night. Apparently Namrata's brother and his wife made a huge scene about her coming late. And they were shocked to see her in her new avatar.

'Namrata's sister-in-law is like a skeleton in clothes. She is *that* thin. And they were obviously dressed to go out somewhere. She was wearing some slinky thing that reached just mid-thigh and you should have seen their faces when they saw her,' Mini recounts.

'God, I hope they're not giving her a hard time!'

'I know. And our girl Namrata was so cowed the moment she saw them that she bent her head and walked in like she was walking into prison,' Mini says.

I wince. Poor thing. 'What about her mother?'

'She came outside to see what was happening and was also shocked at Namrata's haircut.'

'I wish she had a phone so I could call her,' I tell Mini.

'Hang on. I'll text you her home phone number. You can call her on that,' Mini says.

'She gave it to you?' I ask, eyes round in surprise.

'Well, yeah, I asked for her number in the car. She told me with such difficulty that she didn't have a phone,' Mini says.

'She must have been embarrassed.'

'No, it was because she had to speak in front of Vinay. I know for sure. She murmured so softly that I had to ask her again. Then she gave her landline number, which, of course, I asked Vinay to note down since I was driving,' Mini said with a chuckle.

'You are so devious!' I say, surprised. Beneath her brash behaviour and don't-mess-with-me vibe, Mini is either a romantic or she enjoys meddling in other people's lives, a little like me.

'Whatever,' she expels a sigh. 'What are your plans for the weekend?'

'Um, nothing. Maybe shopping with Mom. And we'll probably meet a lawyer for Farida,' I tell her.

'God, I can't believe the nerve of that woman!' Mini says. Reshma Phuppu is really a thorn in Farida's side. I tell Mini the whole story about Farida's parents dying, and Reshma Phuppu and her husband hijacking her life.

'That is so weird. It's like . . .'

'A B-grade Hindi movie. Yes. Farida says the same thing.' I complete her sentence with a smile.

'Why is everyone's life so tough?'

'I have no idea,' I tell her. Actually, mine isn't. It's quite easy-going actually. But I don't want to say anything and jinx it.

We talk a little more and then hang up. I can't stop thinking about Namrata's situation. From next month, she's going to be a full-time employee. I hope things will be better once her family sees she has a stable job.

As I ponder this, I walk out of my room and stop, shell-shocked. Ajay is talking earnestly to Mom and Farida. They can't keep doing this to me. When did he come over? I didn't even hear the doorbell ring. He looks up at me and smiles, and Mom, of course, catches that. I can see her beaming and almost hear the thoughts in her head. But then I look at Farida and lose my train of thought. She has tears in her eyes and yet she's smiling.

'What happened?' I ask, walking over to her quickly.

'Ajay found Irshad,' she says, her voice trembling.

26

'What?' I don't believe it. I can't. Farida has been looking for Irshad for so long. How did Ajay find him in one night?

'Come, sit. I'll explain,' Ajay says. I walk over to them warily and sit down.

'How do you know about him? Farida didn't even tell you about Irshad.'

'That's right. Last night I kept thinking about this whole turn of events,' Ajay starts and I quickly glance at Mom, but she's looking at Ajay like he's some sort of saviour.

'And I did promise to set Farida up with a lawyer,' he continues.

'Irshad is a lawyer?' I jump in and everyone looks at me exasperatedly for interrupting.

'What? I mean, this is just so unbelievable,' I mutter.

Everyone ignores me and Ajay continues, 'So, I texted a couple of lawyer friends and one guy put me in touch with someone who practises family law. One thing led to another.'

'Apparently, someone somewhere in Ajay's network is connected to Irshad, who lives in Mumbai now and is a doctor,' Farida said breathlessly.

'Whoa!'

'How do you know it's him?' I ask, unwilling to accept that it was so easy to find Irshad.

'I don't know, but Ajay got me his number. I'll have to call and find out,' Farida says, her eyes shining. God, this could be such a bad idea if it's not him. And what if it's some impostor? Also, how much can we trust Ajay? We barely know him ourselves.

'Ajay, this is all so fantastical,' I admit finally.

'I know. I can't believe it myself. Irshad is the family doctor of a good friend of mine who used to live in Pune but moved to Mumbai recently,' Ajay says.

'But who brought him up? How did he even come up in the conversation?' I ask.

Ajay nods as though he understands my incredulous expression and pulls out his phone. He opens WhatsApp, taps on a group chat, scrolls up and hands the phone to me. I read the conversations, feeling slightly weird. God, what do thirty-something guys talk about on WhatsApp groups? Ugh! I don't want to know.

But my curiosity is aroused when I read Ajay's message to the group, explaining Farida's situation and how her aunt has taken control of the house. From there, a couple of messages go back and forth about relatives and then someone comments that he knows of another person whose family lost their house to some conniving relatives.

This goes on for a bit until I read the part where Irshad is mentioned. And like he says, it all begins to fall in place.

'Call him!' I urge Farida. I still can't believe it. I need more proof.

'Now?' she asks, looking around at us and blushing. Ajay looks puzzled. He has no idea what Irshad means to her.

'Yes, now. Come, we'll go to your room and talk if you want,' I tell her, catching hold of her elbow and forcing her to get up.

'But . . .' Ajay protests.

'We'll come back and tell you all the details,' I promise and leave him with my mother who begins on the personal questions.

I can sense his eyes on me as I walk away but I don't turn back to look at him. I need some more clarity where he is concerned and I need to talk to Farida about it. But first, we need to check if this man is indeed Irshad.

She sits down on her bed and takes a couple of deep breaths. 'Okay, here goes,' she says and dials the number.

'Speakerphone?' I whisper and she shakes her head. I shake my head again. I need to listen in to see if it really is him. She rolls her eyes and puts the phone on the bed just as the line connects.

'Hello,' a deep male voice answers. Farida's cheeks turn red.

'Irshad?' she manages to squeak.

'Er, who is this?' the voice asks. Farida looks at me, almost hyperventilating.

'It's Farida,' she manages when I prod her to speak.

There's silence at the other end for an agonizing stretch of nearly a minute.

'Who?' the voice asks again, sounding deeply suspicious.

'Farida, your cousin,' she says, looking at me, worried. Maybe this is the wrong Irshad after all.

'How did you get my number and how do you know about Farida?' the voice asks again, this time more firm.

'How we got your number is a long story and she knows about Farida because she *is* Farida,' I cut in, unable to stop myself.

'Who are *you*?' Irshad now sounds even more puzzled.

'Priya. Farida's friend,' I reply.

'Oh my god, it really is you then, Farida?' he asks, and I can sense the wonder and shock in his voice.

'Yes, it is,' she replies softly.

'I thought . . . I came to your house after the accident and that woman told me you'd died too,' he says quickly.

Farida and I look at each other in shock. Reshma Phuppu *met* Irshad? She told him that Farida was dead?

I'm convinced it is him.

27

S till, one last test.

'Do you remember what happened in the guava tree in Farida's house?' I ask.

'How can I forget?' he asks, his voice wry. Farida frowns at me and shakes her head but I grin.

'Do tell,' I continue grinning.

'Both of you got stuck in the top branch and were scared to come down. Priya managed to make it down somehow but scratched her legs badly. Farida was petrified and I had to put her on my back and bring her down. I can't forget how my back hurt after that,' he says.

Farida shuts her eyes in mortification but I'm thrilled. It *really* is him.

'Where were you all these days? How come you're in Mumbai?' I ask.

'I moved back to India when my parents passed away. I was already a doctor by then and I got a good job at a hospital here. I'm a paediatrician,' he says.

Wow.

'When did you come to Bangalore and talk to Reshma Phuppu?' Farida asks.

'A week or so after your parents died. I came with my parents but that woman wouldn't let us into the house. She said your entire family died in the accident and they were living in the house now; that the house had been sold to them. My father wanted to know who sold them the house and they talked for a bit. I was too devastated to hang around and listen to them. I couldn't stop thinking of the summer I visited you. I don't know what she told him or even why he was convinced. There was nothing we could do, so we left,' he says.

'I must have been in school then,' Farida says, tears in her eyes; to think that she'd been so close to living with Irshad and his family.

'I still can't believe this!' he mutters.

'I've been searching for you on Facebook and LinkedIn all these years,' Farida says softly.

'Um, I'm not on either of those. No time,' he admits. 'Farida? Did you call that woman Reshma Phuppu?' he asks.

'Yes. Why? She's my father's cousin and after the accident, she and her husband came to take care of me. Or so she claims,' Farida scoffs.

'I'm pretty sure she's a fraud. I don't think she's your father's cousin. Otherwise why would she lie to me like that?' Irshad speaks urgently. 'Are you with them now? Please tell me you're married and don't live with them.'

Farida's face falls ever so briefly. 'I don't live with them. I'm not married either. I stay with Priya,' she says.

Irshad expels a breath. 'Why are you living with Priya?' he asks.

'Long story,' she murmurs but I can see the frown line etched on her forehead. I know what she wants to ask him but she seems reluctant to do it.

Farida looks at me and shakes her head but I have to ask. We have to know.

'What about you, Irshad? Are you married?' I ask, fingers crossed.

He chuckles. 'No, but I'm engaged. I'm getting married in a few months. It's going to be so cool to have Farida with us for the wedding!'

I squeeze Farida's hand and urge her to continue talking, but it's like she's lost her voice.

'Wow, that's wonderful, Irshad,' I summon some fake cheer. 'You must be awfully busy and we're probably keeping you from saving some child's life. Let's stay in touch, okay? And I hope you come to Bangalore soon.'

'Yes but . . .' he says as I end the call and look at Farida, who has tears in her eyes. I lean forward and hug her.

'Look, it's more important that you found him. That's really nothing short of miraculous,' I tell her.

She nods but I can see that she's already in a funk. I pick up her phone, save the number and refresh WhatsApp, hoping he uses that at least. He does.

'Look,' I tell her, tapping his display picture. Both of us lean in to get a closer look.

Irshad looks nothing like the boy we remember. Although on careful consideration, one can spot traces of him. From the little we can see in the picture, he's traditionally handsome with a square jaw. I can see a bit of grey in his hair which makes him look distinguished. But his eyes are intense, piercing, even in a WhatsApp photo.

Farida puts her phone face down and looks away. 'Can you please thank Ajay on my behalf? I don't think I can come outside and talk now. He must think I'm ungrateful, but I can't thank him enough for what he's done,' she says softly.

Nodding, I get up and leave. As I open the door, I turn to see her pick up the phone and look at Irshad's picture.

28

Ajay is not outside. I don't know what to make of it. I'd expected to see him again so it's a bit of a disappointment.

'Ajay had to leave,' Mom says, also looking disappointed. 'A family member turned up.'

'Oh.'

'Was it Farida's Irshad then?' Mom asks and I nod. Mom can't believe it either. We were Farida's neighbours back then and Mom too had met Irshad. She wanted to take Farida in when her parents died, but Reshma Phuppu had occupied the house. Also, my douchebag father decided to have his affair around the same time, so Mom was preoccupied.

'Is she okay?'

'She is. But she needs a little time,' I tell her. I can't tell her about the enduring crush Farida has had on Irshad. Mom wouldn't understand and, frankly, I don't either. She's nearly thirty and she can't possibly be devastated over this. He was a childhood crush.

Mom and I make plans to go shopping and we hope we'll be able to convince Farida to join us.

'I'm going back on Monday,' Mom announces and I look at her in surprise. Usually, her visits last a week at least.

'How come?' I ask.

'I am going to visit Sheila actually. She's been asking me to come sooner,' she says, referring to her sister, my aunt, who lives in Dehradun.

'Why?' I'm curious because Mom visited her just a few months ago.

'She's got a proposal for Seema and she wants to discuss it with me,' Mom says.

'But Seema is just twenty-four, isn't she? Why does Sheila Maasi want to get her married so early?' I ask, unable to stop myself. My mother frowns.

'Getting married early is not a problem. Getting married late, however . . .' she trails off. Aargh! I walked right into that one.

'Anyhow, I wanted to talk to you and see how you were before I went there. I wanted to see if you were any closer to getting married, now that you'll be thirty in a month.'

'In more than a month,' I counter.

'Well yes. Your brother will be happy to have me out of his hair again I guess, because that means I'll be meddling less in his life,' she says.

Right. She can guess my brother's feelings and intentions but not mine. I don't say anything because that would just mean more fights between us.

I check in on Farida and see that she has fallen asleep. I let her be and head back to my room where I see that Mini has sent me Namrata's landline number. Eager to know if she's okay, I dial the number immediately.

A female voice answers after a few rings. I can sense it's an older woman.

'Who is this?' she asks in Kannada.

'May I speak to Namrata?' I ask. There's silence for a bit and then a slight clunk as the woman places the receiver on a surface. After a short while, a breathless Namrata comes on the phone.

'Hello?'

'Hi, it's Priya,' I tell her.

'Oh hi. How . . . how are you?' she asks.

'Is everything all right at home? I got your number from Mini.'

'I . . . yes . . . actually, yes, things are fine,' Namrata babbles.

'What about your brother and his wife?'

'Well, everyone is shocked about the haircut,' she whispers.

'God, it's just a haircut! No big deal!'

'Yes, but . . . my bhabhi said some mean things about me last night,' she continues, sounding furtive.

'Sticks and stones. Where's she now?'

'They're asleep. They got back late last night from a party.'

'Well, just ignore them and keep doing your thing,' I tell her.

'What thing?' she sounds surprised.

'Well, that thing you were doing yesterday. Holding your own.'

'I . . . I didn't do anything,' she says faintly.

'You did too,' I tell her but don't elaborate and end the call, telling her I'll see her in the office on Monday.

'Shall we go somewhere for brunch and then shopping?' I ask Farida who is still lying in bed, awake now, staring at the ceiling.

'I'm not in the mood. You go with Aunty,' she murmurs.

'Absolutely not. You're coming with us,' I tell her and grab her hand.

'Let it be, Priya,' she protests.

'No. You found Irshad today. It's a day to celebrate!'

'He's getting married soon,' she says in a whisper.

'So? I mean, you can't blame the guy. It's not like he promised he'd marry you or that he cheated on you. He didn't even know you were alive. And even if you feel differently about him, you have to move on,' I tell her, sitting down beside her.

'You're right,' she concedes after a moment.

'Come. Pancakes make everything better,' I promise her. She exhales loudly and we leave the house soon. Mom and Farida walk towards the lift. I'm locking up when Ajay's door opens.

Ajay and Anya step out. Looks like they're going out for the day too. I smile and wave at them and Ajay waves back, but then he steps away from the door and I realize he's making way for someone else. Someone who is dressed in a red silk top and jeans that look like they've been poured on to her body. Someone who bends down to kiss the top of Anya's head. Someone whose rich perfume wafts towards me. The woman straightens up and I gasp. It's Anya's mother.

29

Okay, wait. It's not her. It can't be. But the woman who is standing with Ajay and Anya looks so much like the woman in the photo I'd seen in Ajay's apartment.

'Hey, we were just heading out,' Ajay says with a smile that doesn't reach his eyes. In fact, it looks like he's avoiding looking at me.

'So were we,' I tell him and move towards the lift where Mom and Farida are waiting for me. As I get in, Mom looks at me and then at Ajay who is also heading this way.

'I thought you'd want to take the stairs,' I joke as they enter the lift. Ajay doesn't respond to that and my stomach ties up in knots. I exhale as he pulls the scissor gates together. So much perfume!

'This is Kirti's sister, Natasha,' Ajay explains. Right. His sister-in-law who looks remarkably like his wife. Mom looks at Natasha speculatively.

'Hi,' Natasha responds but without much enthusiasm. Before we can make polite conversation, she turns around to talk to Anya and Ajay about something. She's effectively cut us off. We get out on the ground floor while they stay inside, waiting for the lift to take them to the basement. As I glance back, I can't help but think that they look like a perfect family. Ajay still doesn't look at me.

In the Uber, Mom is silent. Farida is silent. I'm sure I'm not the only one with thoughts churning in my head; I can't stand the silence any longer.

'Mom. What happened? Why are you so quiet?' I ask her.

She looks at me and then shrugs. 'Do you like Ajay?' she asks.

'Why?'

'I just thought . . .'

'What?'

'I really like him. I mean, for you,' she explains flustered.

My cheeks turn hot. Farida is still spaced out, and I need her combination of charm and snarky remarks to turn this around, but it looks like I'm going to have to manage on my own.

'Mom, things don't happen like that, okay? First of all, I don't even know if he's interested and . . .'

'Oh, he is,' Mom confirms.

'Yeah, but . . .'

'And you are too,' she continues.

'What?'

'Yes. This morning when he came home, I told him I'd give him his kulfi but he said you had already given it to him last night,' she says with a sly smile.

'Well, it may not go beyond that, okay? So stop dreaming up all these scenarios where I get married to him. I don't think he's looking for that,' I tell her, furious with Ajay for telling Mom.

'We'll see. But I'm worried about this Natasha now. That girl—'

'Is very pretty,' Farida adds unhelpfully.

Hot, I'd say. She's definitely hot. I mean, *I* felt a bit like salivating in her presence so I can imagine what she does to men. And if that's how beautiful Ajay's wife was, I can see how difficult it must have been for him to get over her. If he ever got over her, that is.

'Don't waste your time, okay,' Mom says. I'm intrigued.

'What do you mean?' Does she mean he's out of my league?

'Well, don't just waste time with him. Get serious, before that Natasha snaps him up.'

'What if I don't want to?' I ask.

'Really? You don't want to?'

'He's not a prize I have to win, okay? I like him and he likes me, but both of us aren't going to rush into anything just because of that. We want to see how things go,' I tell her.

'I knew it,' she says triumphantly.

'What?'

'I knew something was going on between the two of you from the moment he walked into the house. His eyes lit up when he saw you,' she says.

'Oh please.' Could it be true? If his eyes lit up last night, why couldn't he meet my gaze today?

30

On Monday morning, I park the scooter in the office parking lot, already exhausted. I need another weekend just to recover from all the excitement of the past two days. Vinay is heading upstairs, but he stops when he sees me and smiles.

'Hi!'

'Hey!' I'm not really in the mood for conversation but he falls in line with me as we sign in and head upstairs. Vinay makes small talk, praising my mom's food and talking about how lucky he was to be in the same supermarket as Mini on Friday.

'I mean normally I chill with a beer and maybe check out a sports channel if I'm lucky enough to be get home early on a Friday evening,' he goes on while we enter the lift. I don't reply because I don't think I'm expected to. I don't know why he's even talking this much to me. Normally, he's wrapped up in his own life.

As we near my work bay, I realize why he's being this chatty.

'So, this girl Namrata, she works with you? How come I've not seen her around very much?' he asks, genuinely puzzled while his eyes continue to search for her. I snort derisively.

'You just didn't open your eyes, I suppose,' I tell him as I dump my bag on my chair and head to the restroom.

Turns out, several people in the office have discovered Namrata's existence. She walks in, a little later than usual, and I'm thankful she hasn't tied her hair back. It's amazing what a haircut can do. Even though she's wearing her old clothes, she's brimming with confidence now. No more slouching, no more hiding her face behind her hair. Heads turn as she walks in, but Namrata is oblivious to the attention.

'How was your weekend?' I ask her as she places her bag on her desk and smiles at me. Her hair frames her face in soft waves and she looks nearly ten years younger.

'The usual,' she replies as she switches on her system. Mini walks past us and then does a double take when she spots Namrata.

'Well, I'll be damned,' she says as she walks towards us, a chipped coffee mug in her hand.

'What? You already saw her on Friday night,' I say as I open my email.

'Yes, but I didn't expect to see her maintain the look so well. Good on you,' she praises Namrata whose face flushes a little. 'And, oh my god, the sickos in the office think she's a new babe. They've kind of erased the old Namrata from their memories.'

Namrata looks worried.

'Relax. Even Vinay was asking about you,' I tell her. I feel like patting myself on the back. I guess I have Amrita, the back-stabber, to thank.

'What did he say?' She looks petrified.

'Ask him yourself,' I tell her as I spot Vinay walking towards us.

'Shall we step out to the terrace for a bit?' I ask Mini who's been leaning against the desk. She straightens and nods.

'No, no!' Namrata whispers.

'Relax. Just take a deep breath. You managed on Friday, you can manage now too,' I tell her as we leave. I desperately want to know what's happening but it's better to let things unfold first.

Mini is silent on her way up. 'What happened? Are you okay?' I ask her.

She sighs. 'It's Akash. I can't get him out of my head. I mean, I've been thinking about what you guys told me the other day. That maybe he never meant to leave his wife. And . . . I need to know if that's true. I need closure. Then maybe I'll move the fuck on. Quit this job. Even this city.'

The lift doors open and deposit us on to the terrace. We step out and I rub my eyes tiredly. Mom left on a morning flight, which meant I had to wake up at an ungodly hour to book a cab. Afterwards, I was too wired to sleep because I spotted Ajay and Natasha jogging as I headed back up to my apartment. She, of course, ignored me and before Ajay could say anything, she whispered something in his ear, making him turn towards her. I woke up Farida to tell her everything.

Farida, on the other hand, had spent most of the night catching up with Irshad who was on night duty. She was so sleepy and spaced out that she had no clue what I was talking about. So I decided to go back to my room and fret a little more.

Mom had told me she liked Ajay and that I had her blessings (whatever!) to go ahead.

'Go ahead and do what? Seduce him?' I snapped at her as I checked my phone to see when her cab would arrive.

'No, I didn't mean that,' Mom said, scandalized.

'Then?'

'Just talk to him. Spend time with him. With Anya too. Ask about how long this Natasha plans to stay,' she advised. I just gaped at her. Did she really think I could do all this? Ask prying questions about Ajay's sister-in-law?

'*You* should have asked,' I muttered, as finally my phone beeped.

'I know. I should have. Maybe I'll call him and ask,' she said.

'No need. Thank god you don't have his number!' There really was no saying what Mom would do. I'd die of embarrassment if she ever did something like that.

'Of course I have his number,' she said as she entered the cab. 'I took his card the first day we met.'

The uneasy conversation with my mother and then seeing Ajay and Natasha together had really thrown me.

'What do you plan to do?' I ask Mini, vaguely aware that she's been talking about this guy Akash all along.

'I do want to confront him but . . . I don't want things to get ugly. I . . .' She looks lost.

'Didn't you say he was a creative writing teacher?' I ask.

'Yeah? So?'

'How about we enrol Namrata in his class? I think she might be interested in creative writing,' I say, slowly warming up to the idea.

'And how will that help?' Mini asks.

'Well, she could ask around about him. Did his Facebook profile provide any clues about what he's been up to?'

'He's not on Facebook, dude. He doesn't like it. Invasion of privacy, he says. I thought it was cool but now . . .' She trails off. What is it with these guys not being on Facebook, making it so difficult for us to find them, I think with irritation.

'Why the funny face?' she asks. I tell her about Irshad and she's, of course, really surprised.

'Wow! That was some dinner party your mom threw,' she jokes.

'Tell me about it. Do you think we should go down and see what's happened?' We've been up here for fifteen minutes now.

'Yeah. I have work to do too. So, we enrol Namrata in Akash's class and then what? She spies on him for us? I mean, I think it would be better if you did it, no?' Mini asks as we head back to the lift.

'Me? I'm not interested in writing at all. But yeah, we might have to wait a bit before we do this.'

'Why?'

'Well, these things cost money, right? She won't let either of us pay for the course,' I remind her.

'Oh . . . then . . .'

'Just wait a couple of months. Let her get some money of her own. We'll make sure she doesn't give it all to her mother or brother. Then we can broach the topic with her,' I advise Mini.

'Even if we get her into the course, do you think *she* can spy on Akash? Find out what went wrong? I might as well just talk to him but he's blocked my number.' Mini looks down as she says this.

'*He* blocked *your* number?' I ask, surprised.

'I kind of went overboard and called him around a hundred times when we broke up,' she confesses. I don't know what to say. Mini has always come across as a strong feminist and this kind of stalker behaviour doesn't fit with that image at all. She looks a bit abashed and I feel bad for judging her even if just for a second.

'It happens, I guess,' I tell her as the lift doors open. She shakes her head furiously.

'No, this kind of thing never happens with me. I can love 'em and leave 'em but what I had with Akash was so special. I just . . .' She breaks away and takes a deep breath. 'Fine, I'll wait for a while. I just hope Namrata can actually pull it off.'

I shrug. 'No harm in trying.'

'That girl used to be scared of her own shadow,' Mini reminds me. 'But if she manages to do this, then maybe I can . . . try to move on.'

'We'll see,' I tell her, walking back to my desk, hoping against hope that Namrata didn't run away to the restroom when faced with Vinay.

Thankfully, she's still in her place. She looks up at us, her eyes wide.

'What happened?' I ask, concerned.

'Vinay asked me out for lunch,' she says in a hushed whisper.

31

'You may be meddlesome, but I'm a freaking genius,' Mini proclaims as she turns to me.

Namrata looks at us, puzzled.

'What?' she says, her voice trailing away faintly.

'Never mind. What did you tell him?' I ask her.

She blushes. 'I just nodded. But I'm terrified. What will we even talk about? I don't even know him!' she mutters.

'Yet you've been crushing on him ever since you got here,' I whisper. She turns redder.

'Can you blame me?' she asks softly.

Mini rolls her eyes. 'Someone got a tongue along with a makeover,' she says.

'When are you going out?' I intervene.

'Today. It's just a casual lunch,' she says quickly.

'That was fast,' I tell her. Mini leaves after a while, saying she has a shitload of work to complete.

Namrata and I get back to work but she obviously can't focus. The copy for the blog post she sends me is riddled with typos, and it's not like her at all. During our mid-morning coffee break, she looks at me, all tense.

'I don't know why I said yes,' she whispers. 'What was I thinking? I don't know anything. What if he wants to talk about sports with me? I don't watch cricket!'

'Firstly, I'm sure guys don't want to talk sports when they're out on a lunch date and, secondly, he's into football, not cricket,' I tell her.

'Like that helps me,' she mutters. I try hard not to smile. It's actually impossible to believe that the mousy, quiet girl from last week has been replaced by this person.

Soon enough, it's lunchtime and she turns to me, terrified. 'I think I'm going to throw up,' she says.

'No. You're not. Just take deep breaths,' I advise her.

Suddenly, her eyes grow round. 'Didn't Vinay have to talk to the HR manager about his relationship with Radhika? What if he does the same now? Ambrish is my mother's cousin,' she says.

I try to calm her down. 'First of all, it's a lunch date, that's it. You don't need the HR manager's permission for that. And so what if this guy tells your mother? You're nearly thirty. Own it, girl!'

'Who's nearly thirty?'

Both of us turn around. Vinay is looking at us, puzzled. When did *he* come?

'Um, both of us,' I tell him. 'We're both turning thirty soon.'

He looks so taken aback, it's almost funny.

'What's wrong?' I ask him.

'I . . . I didn't know . . .' He trails off. Oh my god, is he serious? He has a problem with Namrata turning thirty? I look at Namrata, who as usual is slow on the uptake.

I stare at Vinay and he shuffles his feet, hands in his pockets. 'Ready?' he asks Namrata, who nods. I watch them leave with a great deal of misgiving. She's going to be hurt by the end of this. I'm sure. She's too naive and sweet and, apparently, a little too old for Vinay.

Mini joins me for lunch and I tell her what happened. She is pretty angry too.

'What does age have to do with anything?' she bursts out.

'You tell me,' I reply, mentally adding one more thing to hate about the number thirty.

32

While Namrata is away, I call up Farida to see how she's doing. She sounds upbeat.

'Irshad says he's definitely coming to Bangalore soon,' she says.

'Oh good. With his wife? No wait, fiancée, right?'

There's silence. 'Don't be mean, Priya,' she says finally.

I exhale loudly. Everyone's love life is truly fucked up. Apart from Namrata's. But I have a feeling lunch won't go too well.

'I'm not being mean. I'm just being realistic. You have to start thinking of him as just your distant cousin now. That's it. Nothing else,' I tell her.

'I can't! He's . . . I . . .' She's at a loss for words.

'You don't even know what he's like now,' I tell her gently. 'He has a life of his own.'

'Yes and he sounds perfect and amazing. Last night, when he was on night duty, he hung up in the middle of our conversation, saying he'd call back. Naturally I waited. But an hour later, when he didn't, I called. It was nearly 2 a.m. One of his patients, a ten-year-old, was afraid of sleeping in the ward, so he sat beside him and held the little boy's hand until he fell asleep.'

Oh wow. I guess I'd fall in love with someone like that too.

'You're just making things difficult for yourself. He doesn't see you that way. Try to get that in your head,' I tell her, feeling exasperated.

We end the call on an unsavoury note. I actually wanted to ask her if she could check what Natasha was up to, but I couldn't possibly ask her for a favour now that she was pissed at me.

I watch Namrata return to her desk, and I feel deflated as I catch the look on her face. She seems confused and sad. What did that idiot Vinay do?

'He didn't say a word to me during lunch,' she says, still looking baffled.

'Maybe he got tongue-tied and confused,' I offer. She shakes her head.

'He got a call and was on his phone the whole time, all through lunch,' she says.

'That's the problem with these young guys,' I tell her with a huff.

'Young guys?'

'He's just twenty-seven, I think.'

Her face falls. 'Oh. So he heard I'm thirty . . .'

I shrug.

'Okay,' she says softly.

'Okay what?'

'Nothing. I just understood his behaviour. I'm such a tube light,' she says, shaking her head sadly.

'He's an ass. And quite a few guys have asked you out,' I remind her. She has been showing me emails from some of the men who have apparently just realized she exists.

'But I'm not interested in them. I mean, they've just noticed me because I look different. Before this they thought I was part of the furniture,' she says.

So did Vinay. But I don't voice the thought.

'Actually, even Vinay didn't notice me until that evening in your house,' she remembers. 'So, he's no different. All these guys, they're just interested in outward appearances.'

'You were also interested in his outward appearance, right?' I remind her. Her face flushes a little, but she doesn't say anything.

For the rest of the day, we work in silence. Great. At home, Farida isn't talking to me. Here, Namrata won't. With these thoughts chasing each other in my head, I'm unable to concentrate on work. So, I post a passive-aggressive message on Farida's Facebook page.

About ten minutes later, I get a call from my boss who wants to see me in his cabin right away.

33

I usually avoid thinking about my boss, Arvind Kanakadasa. I try to pretend he doesn't exist. It's hard when I have to spend an hour or so in meetings with him every other day. But still, I try.

My boss is a raconteur. His word, not mine. I often wonder if he's taken his surname seriously because Kanakadasa was a famed sixteenth-century Kannada poet and philosopher. However, what it means for me is that he likes to tell long drawn-out stories that have a lesson at the end. Not too different from the moral values classes I had in school. Only, here the lessons have to do with ROI and investor mindset.

I avoid looking at his face as much as possible because . . . well . . . his mouth often purses up in this funny way that reminds me of something rude and I can't get the image out of my head. And he doesn't like it when we laugh *before* he delivers the punchlines to his stories.

Today, he starts off about a boy who copied from the person sitting next to him during an exam without realizing that he was a senior writing a history paper, while the boy had a biology exam. Apparently, the school liked to mix up students to prevent cheating and this boy had copied blindly.

'When the results came in . . .' At this point, Arvind pauses and looks at me expectantly, waiting for me to fill in the blanks.

'Err . . . he got into trouble?' I complete.

'Absolutely,' he says softly. I make plans in my head to order food tonight while Arvind drones on. I'm feeling cranky and am in no mood for Parvati akka's tired sabzi and chapatti. Particularly since Farida is still pissed with me.

'Priya!' he says sharply, and I jump out of my skin.

'Yes, yes. I know,' I say before I realize something is off. He's not in his vomit-inducing gyan-giving mood. In fact, he's angry. That's when he beckons me closer.

He points to his laptop screen. My eyes screw up in concentration as I see the funny-ish passive-aggressive meme I'd posted on Farida's page. I gasp when I see I've posted it from the Citron company account and not my personal one.

I can't believe I've done something so stupid. Something I warn all the interns to be extra careful about. When I posted on Farida's wall, I forgot to switch to my personal Facebook account. So it looks like Citron posted a passive-aggressive message on an unknown person's wall. My boss found out immediately because he received a notification as soon as the post went up. And now I'm sitting in front of him, ready to hear the lecture of a lifetime.

'I'll delete it right away,' I tell him, itching to run back to my system and undo the damage. But he shakes his head.

'Sit,' he says and I comply, most uncomfortably. How could I make such a rookie mistake?

'It was a mistake,' I tell him. He doesn't say anything.

'You know you control Citron's public image. And yet you did this.'

My mouth is completely dry. I have no words to defend myself.

'Priya, I heard you fired two interns long before their internship ended. What's going on?' he asks.

'They were useless and wasted too much time, Arvind. There was a lot of negativity in the office with them around. They were bullying Namrata and they didn't show me any respect,' I babble.

'You need to earn respect,' he says, standing up and going to the whiteboard. No, I groan mentally. I *do not* need a management lesson now. I wish I'd set up the company account on my phone so I could have made the change right away but I'd wanted to avoid situations just like these.

Arvind then proceeds to make a complicated drawing on the whiteboard, turning to me, talking, waving his hands and, nearly half an hour later, he returns to his seat.

'The girl you fired, Amrita? She's coming back but in HR this time,' he says.

What?

'She was a good candidate. I'm surprised you didn't get along with her. You need to be more professional, Priya,' he says, swivelling his chair to face his screen once more.

I don't know how to reply, so I stay silent.

'And fix this mistake please,' he says and tunes me out. I walk back to my desk, feeling like a zombie.

34

It's just Monday but I'd like the week to end already. In the evening, as I'm getting ready to leave, the dupatta wrapped around my face in preparation for the evening traffic, I spot Vinay heading out as well. I call out his name, my voice all muffled and start walking towards him. He stops and turns and his eyes widen, almost in fright. I realize that with my face covered completely and only my eyes visible, he has no clue who I am. I probably look like a *bhootni*.

'It's me, Priya,' I tell him, pulling down the dupatta a little to free my mouth.

He looks uncomfortable. 'I was just heading out to get something to eat. We never get to leave as early as you guys.'

'Oh please. Stop cribbing. Why did you behave like that with Namrata?' I ask him outright.

He is visibly flustered. 'What do you mean? I didn't say anything,' he protests.

'Exactly. You take a girl out for lunch and then ignore her completely. What is she to make of it?'

He looks away uncomfortably. 'I . . . I didn't know that . . .'

'She's almost thirty? Yes. We all are. So? What's the big deal?' I snap at him. It's not like she's turning forty and, even if she were, so what, I think viciously.

'Look, I really don't know what I was thinking when I asked her out, okay? I don't want to get involved with anyone so soon after my break-up, but all that talk in the office was getting to me. I had to see who this girl was and then I saw her at your party and . . . now I'm not so sure,' he says, shrugging.

'Asshole,' I mutter angrily and walk back to my scooter. I'm pretty angry all the way back home. I stop the scooter at the store near my building to get some more peanut butter, hoping it might cheer me up. Almost wistfully, I remember meeting Ajay here for the first time. Was it only last week? It seems like I've known him for longer.

'It's okay. Let her get it.'

'No. It's not okay.'

I freeze. That sounds like Ajay. I look around the aisles and spot him arguing with Natasha, who is holding a big bag of nachos. Anya is pulling at Ajay's hand.

I step back, not willing to witness more of their we're-already-a-family scenes. I want to get away quickly. This time, I'm not buying anything else and the peanut butter will easily go into my handbag. At the cash counter, I pay quickly and am stepping out when I hear my name.

'Priya Aunty!' It's Anya. I wince at the aunty bit. Slowly, I turn around and paste a smile on my face. Ajay and Natasha are right behind her; Ajay is holding a basket with all his shopping.

'Hi Anya!' I address her before looking up at the adults. Natasha seems to have forgotten who I am and Ajay re-introduces us. My smile seems frozen and forced.

'Right. You're one of the chicks next door,' she says. Anya giggles.

'Chicks?' she whispers and I smile back.

'See you guys around,' I say, walking away, when Ajay calls out. Reluctantly, I turn around again.

'You're heading home, right? I want to drop in for a bit,' he says, shifting the shopping basket from one hand to the other.

'Why?' I ask, looking at Natasha instead, who seems bored.

'I never gave you the number of the lawyer. For Farida,' he adds.

'Sure,' I tell him and leave. I walk quickly, making sure I reach the lift before them. I'm inside my apartment two minutes later, somewhat hurt and confused.

Farida isn't home. She usually texts me before leaving, but I guess she's still angry about what I said about her and Irshad. Well, I'm a little pissed at her too. The doorbell rings and I sigh. I haven't even washed up yet.

I open the door and let Ajay in. He looks around for Farida.

'She's not home. You can give me the contact details,' I tell him. We're both standing and I don't feel like inviting him in to sit down.

'Um, sure. I need to talk to you,' he tells me, looking in the direction of the sofa.

'Can you wait for a few minutes? I need to wash up,' I tell him, heading towards my room, feeling self-conscious all of a sudden. My hands are grimy from riding in traffic, but the truth is, I need a minute to compose myself. I'm really happy on the inside to see him but I'm also confused about the whole Natasha thing.

'Shall I make coffee?' he calls out. I roll my eyes. Sure, make yourself at home. No boundaries.

'Okay,' I call out as I peel off my clothes and step into the bathroom for the fastest shower of my life. I towel myself dry and quickly put on whatever I can find. He's waiting in the hall with two mugs of steaming coffee. On second thoughts, forget boundaries; I could get used to this.

'Thanks,' I mutter, as I sink into the sofa and fold my legs a little awkwardly.

We sip the coffee in silence and then he speaks. 'Natasha came for the weekend. She took leave from work and stayed back today. She's leaving now,' he informs me.

I nod but don't say anything.

'It's always a sucker punch when I see her. She looks so much like Kirti, you know,' he mutters.

What can I say?

'She helped me out a lot when Kirti died. I don't think I could have functioned without their help. My wife's family, I mean. They took over and managed everything until I came to grips with my life,' he explains.

Why is he telling me all this?

'My father-in-law actually suggested that I marry Natasha,' he blurts out. My eyes nearly fall out of my head.

'I said no,' he says quickly. 'It's ridiculous. I can't marry her. But they'd spoken to her and for some reason she was okay with it. Now she keeps trying to show me that we'd be good together.'

'How?' I finally manage to squeak out.

'Like this weekend,' he replies immediately. 'She ambushed my weekend and . . .'

'And what?' I'm almost afraid of his answer.

'Nothing. I told her last night that she has a bright future ahead of her. She needs to focus on that and not on a tired old man like me,' he says with a smile.

Oh please. Tired old man, my foot. If I don't see him like that, there's no way Natasha does. And she's known him longer.

'What did she say?' I ask.

'Nothing. She thinks she can make me change my mind, but she can't.' He puts his coffee mug down with finality.

'Why not?' I ask, taken aback when he comes to sit next to me. He takes my mug and places it on the table as well.

'There's no room in my life for anyone else. Just you,' he says, framing my face with his warm hands. I take a deep breath. There's so much I want to tell him, ask him. I'm so confused, especially about what he'd said the other night about his wife's picture. But now is not the time.

I move in closer, feeling considerably better than I had all weekend and all of today. His lips touch mine and his arm goes around me to pull me closer. The last thought in my head before I forget everything else and get lost in the moment is a silent plea to Farida not to return in the next ten minutes at least.

35

'Are you sure this is the right place?' I ask Farida as I stop my scooter outside a yellowing building that must have been off-white a few decades ago.

'That's what Google Maps shows me,' she says, pulling off her helmet. I stash hers in the storage of the scooter and, holding on to mine, walk towards the building.

'You don't have to do this,' she mutters. Farida wanted to see the lawyer alone, but I insisted she wait for the weekend so I could accompany her.

'I want to,' I tell her. The truth is, I'm feeling a little guilty. Farida has stopped talking to me about Irshad, but I can't stop her from seeing what's happening with Ajay. True to his word, Natasha left that evening, and we've been seeing each other regularly since then—coffee, dinner, and walks around the complex at night. Farida offered to babysit Anya a couple of times. Once we all went out together, Farida too. I haven't been this happy in a long time and it makes me feel guilty because she isn't. I can't do a thing about Irshad, but I can help her with the house situation.

We climb the dusty, paan-stained steps of the building to the first floor. It has an open space in the middle so the courtyard and the floors above are also visible. A rusty metal railing runs around the outer section of the corridor and there's a general sense of disuse. We look ahead at the long line of doors, each facing the railing. Farida and I walk single file until we reach the one with a plaque that says 'Mr Raghuvendra' followed by a string of law degrees. We knock and wait.

'Come in,' a gravelly voice calls out. We enter a small square room that is suffocating and smells musty. The walls are covered with wooden cupboards that have either yellowing papers or dusty books stuffed into them. In front of us is a desk behind which sits a diminutive, balding man. I lose all confidence in him immediately. What was Ajay even thinking? He'd seen Reshma Phuppu, right? If we ever went to court, she'd just sit on this guy and he'd be flattened like a tube of toothpaste. I shake my head to rid myself of these ridiculous thoughts.

We sit down and Farida narrates everything to him, including the part about Reshma Phuppu convincing Irshad's family that she was dead and the house had been sold.

'I just want my house back,' Farida says softly. Mr Raghuvendra nods and rocks back and forth in his chair.

'You must have the house deeds?' he asks suddenly.

'Err . . . no,' she says.

'What? You don't know where your house deeds are?' I ask her, shocked. It's never occurred to me to ask her this before. I'd just assumed she had them.

She shrugs. 'I've looked for them everywhere. In my father's study, in my parents' bedroom, but I don't know where the papers are.'

'Find them. Sell the house. Best way to get rid of them,' he offers.

What?

'But . . . I don't want to sell the house,' she protests. She looks upset. I've broached the topic with her earlier as well, asking her to sell the house because it's such a huge encumbrance and also because selling the house would mean Reshma Phuppu would have to go. But I didn't know about the missing deeds.

'I don't see any other way around this. If you take them to court, it's going to be long and messy and you never know how devious relatives can be. You've said that your aunt, this woman, accused you of trying to seduce her husband. There's no saying what they will do to keep the house. I've seen people kill each other over land and property. Don't take chances,' he advises.

It's the advice I've been giving Farida all along, I think. A chunk of the money she gets every month goes to Reshma Phuppu and her husband. I've always been worried about what they would do to get their hands on more money. The possibilities are terrifying. I've seen enough *Crime Patrol* on TV to justify my concerns.

Farida, however, has been hoping for some sort of magic solution to her problem which would involve getting rid of them while keeping the house. Knowing that this isn't going to happen disheartens her further.

If Farida has to sell the house, she needs to find the deeds. And for that, she needs to go to that house and look for them. She won't do it while Reshma Phuppu's asshole husband is still there.

'We are really stuck,' she says as we get on the scooter. 'I was hoping I'd be able to move back into my place. It's been so long since I've lived there,' she says loudly, over the traffic.

I steer the scooter to the side of the road and stop. I take off my helmet and turn to face her. 'You know you can stay with me as long as you want, right? What's the hurry?'

The frown line on her forehead becomes prominent. 'I . . . I don't know. I feel like I've wasted enough time already,' she mutters. Since she doesn't have anything to add, I restart the scooter and we continue towards the apartment.

At home, her phone rings when she's in the loo and I look at the screen. It's Irshad. I'm not really sure why I answer it. He's naturally surprised to hear me. I quickly tell him everything about the house situation because I know Farida won't.

'He did what?' Irshad asks softly when I tell him about how Reshma Phuppu's husband tried to molest Farida.

'Please don't tell her any of this. She's really depressed and she'll be angry if she knows I told you,' I say. There's silence.

'I can't promise that, Priya,' he says finally, sounding angry. 'But one thing is sure. I'm coming to Bangalore very soon.'

'Oh, that would be great!' I exclaim and only then realize that, given the way Farida feels about him, seeing him in person may just complicate things even further. I end the call soon after and delete it from the call history just in case. I put Farida's phone back the way it was just as she emerges from the loo.

I message Ajay to tell him that I won't be meeting him for dinner as Farida needs me. We settle down to watch a show on Netflix and don't speak much. I'm thinking of what will happen when Irshad shows up, when she meets him in person. She's going to be devastated when he leaves. I glance at her staring at the screen and wonder if it was a mistake to involve Irshad. She's going to be so mad at me. She looks at me and raises her eyebrows.

'What?'

'Nothing,' I tell her. Let Irshad come and then we can worry about it.

36

'The annual office party is on Saturday, 5 August,' Arvind announces during one of his regular bore-you-to-death meetings a few days later.

'But don't we always have it on 10 August?' I ask, surprised and confused. 5 August is my birthday.

'Yes, but we have an important client who will be in India at the time and we thought it would be nice to show her the synergy between our teams. I need you to come up with a party plan with a wow factor,' he says. I groan mentally.

Arvind tosses out these words regularly. Often, I have no idea what they mean. I sigh loudly and he looks at me sharply.

'All okay?' he asks.

'Why do you want me to organize it? It's a big event and it's usually handled by an event planning agency, right?' I ask.

'Not this time. We're cutting unnecessary costs. And we're hosting it on the terrace, here in the office,' he says.

'But . . .'

'Priya, I know you'll do a great job. I mean, who else can I turn to? You know how boring everyone else is here,' he says with a smile. He thinks I don't know what he's doing—making me feel like I am a part of a special group while getting me to do things that don't fall under my regular duties.

'It's a lot of work, Arvind, and—'

'And you can do it. You have no idea how much all these software engineers look forward to the party. They've slogged their butts off the entire year. This is when they can legitimately have fun,' he says with a beaming smile.

I've been slogging my butt off too. And I still have to put together this party? In less than a month? Not fair.

'Come up with a fantabulistic theme, okay?' he says, waving his hands around expansively and I cringe. That is not even a word. 'Think outside the box.'

I head back to my work bay feeling angry and somewhat exploited. Namrata looks up, concerned. She's changed so much in the past month and it never ceases to surprise me.

When she got her first pay cheque, I convinced her to keep some money for herself and not hand over everything to her mother. Then I convinced her to go shopping with me. With the new haircut and wardrobe, she's a veritable head-turner, a fact that she still doesn't register.

I update her about what Arvind wants and she gets excited. 'We're organizing it? Our team?' she says, clapping her hands lightly.

'Why are you so excited?' I ask, irritated. 'These parties are terrible. And we won't be able to enjoy ourselves.'

'I don't mind. You can count on me,' she says. Later, during lunch, I explain all of this to Mini, who frowns first and then snorts.

'You two are going to be working while the rest of us get drunk! Ha ha!' she proclaims. I make a face at her. I wouldn't say we're the best of friends now but the three of us have developed a bond over the past month and we end up having lunch together every day.

Suddenly, Namrata stiffens slightly before relaxing. She still has a visceral reaction whenever Vinay is around. Mini and I notice but, as usual, we don't say anything. Mini, of course, feels Namrata should take up the several other offers and go out with someone. We'd discussed this once at my apartment when Mini and Namrata had come over and we had binge-watched *Master of None* on Netflix.

'I don't want to,' Namrata insisted, not looking away from Aziz Ansari on the screen.

'But why not? It's not like Vinay was such fantastic company that every other man will fall short for you,' Mini asked.

'It's not like that. I'm here to do my job and that's what I will do,' she said.

'Let her be,' Farida spoke up, taking her side. I looked at Mini and both of us knew exactly what the other was thinking. Farida perfectly understood Namrata because she too was fixated on one man, no matter how unattainable. And, as usual, she turned on Mini.

'You're one to talk. Why haven't you moved on from Akash?' she asked. Mini's expression turned thunderous.

'Because unlike the two of you, I actually had a relationship and it's not so easy to just get over it and move on,' she snapped back. I avoided looking at her because she'd been pestering me about when we could get Namrata enrolled in the class so she could spy on Akash. I was regretting giving her the idea. I should have encouraged her to just confront him and get it over with, but I thought she'd have a hard time recovering from a face-to-face meeting with him. Now she was like a dog with a bone, constantly asking me to broach the subject with Namrata. I honestly don't know if Namrata would be interested.

'Isn't 5 August your birthday?' Namrata asks as she finishes the last of her gulab jamun and places the plastic cup on her plate.

'Yes.'

'Oh, fuck no! Now that really sucks,' Mini says. 'Were you planning something for your birthday?'

Actually, I had been. I had thought Ajay and I could go out for dinner if Farida was okay babysitting Anya. And we could finally take our hot make-out sessions on sofas, which had become a regular feature over the past few days, to the next level.

Now I'll be the only sober person on my birthday, arranging cabs for all the drunk employees so they reach home safely.

37

'What do you think about joining a creative writing class?' I ask Namrata after Mini has harassed me enough. She looks surprised at first and then very interested and thoughtful.

'Will I get a certificate?' she asks and I'm taken aback. It had never occurred to me to ask Mini about any of these details.

'It depends. Why?' I ask her cautiously.

'If I get a certificate, maybe I can ask the company to pay for it as it will add to my skills here,' she explains. I look at her, surprised. Why hadn't I thought of that?

'But you're not just going for the certificate, are you? You did mention once that you were interested in writing,' I say. It would make me feel like less of a manipulator if she actually wants to join the class.

'Yes, I do. I want to better my writing skills,' she says and goes back to staring at her screen.

'Okay, let me check about this certificate and get back to you,' I tell her and quickly text Mini.

Mini takes a while to reply. She doesn't check her phone as often as I do. 'Yes, they do give out certificates but I was so involved with Akash, I didn't bother to collect mine,' she answers.

When I inform Namrata of this, she immediately looks up the class online. She even registers for the next batch, which starts the following week. It's a weekend-only class, specifically for professionals like her.

My phone buzzes with a text from Farida. She's got a freelance gig to shoot pictures for a friend's wedding in Mumbai. I groan mentally.

'It's perfect. I'll get to meet Irshad too,' she writes. And fall in love with him.

I don't reply immediately, although I'm itching to remind her that he's engaged. She'll just get mad and not talk to me for days.

'When are you going?' I type back finally.

'4 August,' she replies. Great. Looks like the universe really wants to screw with my birthday plans. Of course, now there's no way Ajay and I could . . . could . . . never mind.

Ajay and I haven't had the big talk yet. It keeps niggling at the back of my mind. He's perfect in so many ways and I really like him. He's funny and goofy but can also be serious and forbidding when the occasion arises. I caught him once in a suit and thought he looked hot—all distant and aloof. When he spotted me, he grinned widely, diluting the effect considerably.

There have been times in the park with Anya when he's had to answer a call from work apologetically. Oh, I *love* seeing him go into work mode because then a frown line appears on his forehead and he doesn't focus on his immediate surroundings. His voice and demeanour change considerably

and it is *such* a turn-on. He's only vaguely aware of me as he
barks commands on the phone and refuses to take no for an
answer. Once he ends the call, he is back to being the warm
and lovable guy I know. I wonder what it would take for him
to be like that with me . . .

There was also the time I went to his apartment to return
something and Anya opened the door. Usually, she's not
allowed to open the door but this time she'd heard my voice.
Ajay hadn't heard the bell and had walked into the living
room, hair wet from a shower, towel around his hips, singing
an old Govinda song softly, '*Meri* pant *bhi* sexy, meri shirt bhi
sexy.' He stopped short when he saw me in the hallway. The
expression on his face was priceless, especially when I nodded
gravely and whispered softly, '*Tera* chest bhi sexy, *tere* legs bhi
sexy.' Thankfully Anya had disappeared into her room by
then.

'I'll show you sexy,' he growled, shaking his wet hair and
catching me before I could run away. He held me close, his
arm around my waist, and the expression on his face serious.
The laughter died on my lips when I trailed my hands over his
hard chest and abs but had to force myself to stop exploring
further because Anya could come out at any moment.

I've managed to spend a bit of time with Anya as well.
She's chirpy and funny and says whatever is on her mind,
which is often not polite, leaving Ajay to handle the aftermath.
Once we passed by a woman who was taking an evening walk,
striding away righteously, puffing loudly.

'Why is that aunty so fat?' she'd asked loudly. The woman
thankfully didn't hear her and Ajay and I quickly took her
home before she could get us into any more trouble. So while

I enjoy my time with Ajay, I also look forward to talking to Anya.

But. We still need to talk about where this is going. He'd told me right at the beginning that he's not into random hook-ups and neither am I. I'm tired of all that anyway. I just want a guy who is trustworthy and good, and seeing Ajay with Anya confirms all that for me, many times over. I'm not fond of labels but what do we call this?

And that photo of his wife in the living room. His words that day are seared into my brain. He felt *safe* displaying it. He needs to explain what that means but I fear it'll sound weird if I bring it up randomly. I'd hoped that we would clear all these things on my birthday and then proceed to . . . you know . . .

I look down at my phone and see that Farida's left a few messages already.

I'm not going to tell him I'm in Mumbai. I'm going to surprise him.

What do you think?

Bad idea, I think, but don't tell her in so many words. Instead I resort to what everyone who wants to escape an uneasy conversation does—emojis.

I get back to work and start making a list of things we'll need for the party. Arvind has given me such short notice and I have loads to do—organize lists of people's food choices, send them around and get confirmations, hire a caterer, organize some sort of entertainment . . . I shake my head in despair.

It's late by the time I finish up. Well, late by my standards. The software guys are still prowling the office like ghouls with bad hair and overgrown beards. They always get like this, right before a release. One of the clients wanted them to build an entirely new accounting product for their company. Normally, clients are happy with basic customization—their company logos and colours on the user interface. But this one had several other requirements and Arvind was happy charging them ridiculous amounts of money while the software engineers and the designers slogged, testing and releasing the new product.

I look around me. Namrata could have left an hour ago but she stuck around to help me out. She's hunched over her system looking for interesting entertainment that we can get cheaply when I spot Vinay walking across the bay towards the coffee machine. He glances in our direction and slowly comes to a halt, his gaze on Namrata, as she absently gathers her hair and pushes a pencil through it to hold the makeshift bun in place. I have no idea what's going on in his mind as he continues to look at her before walking away.

38

Time just slips past me and before I even know it, 31 July is here. I've mostly organized everything but I'm still nervous. Arvind keeps making pointed references to my supposedly excellent party-planning abilities and it takes all my will power not to throw something at him. I know how this works—if the party sucks, I will be blamed and if it's amazing, he'll take the credit.

When Namrata joined the creative writing class, I'd told her tentatively about our initial plan of spying on Akash. She was mortified and upset and had refused to do anything of the sort. But Mini had told her that she needed to think like a friend and help her out.

'I need closure and you can help me get it, dammit!' she'd said finally, to which Namrata had agreed reluctantly. She's been to two classes so far and hasn't been able to do anything even close to spying. Mini keeps coming over to our work bay to ask us but Namrata has no answers and I can sense Mini's frustration growing.

'What does she expect me to find out anyway?' Namrata asks me after Mini leaves in a huff on one such occasion. I shrug.

'You know, if he was stringing her along all this time,' I suggest.

'And how do I find that out? I can't just go and ask him outright,' Namrata says.

True. 'Have you got the final count of people for the party?' I ask her, glancing over her shoulder to see the Excel sheet she's been working on.

'Yes, almost. Just a couple more people have to confirm their plus ones. One guest per employee, right?' she asks.

'Yes. Why? Do you want to call your mother?' I ask jokingly but she's considering it seriously.

'I don't know. She . . . she'll feel out of place. What about you? Are you bringing Ajay or Farida?'

'Eh. Neither. I'll be too busy to actually enjoy the party, you know. And Farida is headed to Mumbai that week for a wedding photography gig.'

A little later, downstairs in the parking lot just as I'm leaving, Mini catches hold of me.

'Look, dude. My dad has been asking me to visit him in Hong Kong,' she says.

'Whoa. Lucky you,' I tell her, arranging the dupatta over my mouth.

'Yeah, I'm not sure I want to go. He keeps posting stuff on Instagram that makes me cringe and I don't think I want to see it in person,' she says, swinging her car keys around her forefinger.

'Oh, like what?' I ask her, pulling the dupatta down, mentally making a note to follow her father on Instagram. She apparently reads the thought on my transparent-as-water face and scowls.

'Don't even think about it,' she growls. I shrug. 'He posts pics of him with the girls he's with. I'd say it was annoying but it's more disgusting.'

Oh. 'I *won't* follow him. What did you want?' I ask her. Namrata is just coming down the stairs and she looks at the two of us. I wave her over.

'Hi,' she says. 'I need to rush or I'll miss the bus. I'll talk to you guys tomorrow?'

We watch her as she hurries away. 'Some makeover, huh?' Mini comments.

'I didn't do anything. She came out of her shell on her own. Anyway, what did you want?'

'Look, I wanted to ask Namrata if I could accompany her to class next time. I want to do this and maybe . . . take a leave of absence and visit my father. A change of scene will be good for me,' she says. I frown and shake my head.

'Going to class with Namrata is not a good idea. Anyway, I think she's skipping the next class as it is on the day of the party,' I tell her.

Mini crosses her arms. 'What do you mean it's not a good idea? What can go wrong?' she shrugs.

'Everything. Will it really be good for you to see him again?'

'I'll get closure.'

'Maybe he decided he didn't want to leave his wife for you after all,' I tell her with a wince.

Mini narrows her eyes. 'Yes, but he should have told me, right?'

'Um, maybe he was intimidated by you?' I suggest, hoping she won't bite my head off for saying it.

'What? By me? Akash was the only guy who wasn't. Don't you think I would recognize that in a man?' she asks, lowering her gaze.

'Look, you were in a relationship with a married man. There's no scenario in which that ends well.'

Her nostrils flare a little. 'Whatever. Tell Namrata I'm going with her on Saturday,' she says and stalks off.

God, she really is a bully sometimes. I get on my scooter and ride away, feeling stressed and annoyed.

At home, Farida is running around as though she's going to Mumbai the very next day. She's excited and hyper and is talking on and on.

'What about when you come back from Mumbai?' I ask her.

'What do you mean?'

'Have you thought about how you'll feel?'

'Priya, what are you talking about?' she asks, standing in front of the mirror, holding a white chikan kurti against herself.

'You're going to meet Irshad and when you come back . . .'

'I'll be fine,' she says easily.

I shake my head. 'No, you won't. You're going to be a mess. Shouldn't you be searching for your house deeds instead?' I ask her.

'How? I can't go back to the house when they're there. And I won't be a mess. I'll be fine.'

I meet her eyes in the mirror and know she's lying. It's like she's determined to self-destruct and I can't do anything but stand by and watch.

39

On 1 August, Farida gets a call that changes everything. The wedding photography gig has been cancelled. The bride has found a local photographer with better credentials and they call up Farida to awkwardly inform her. Naturally, Farida goes into a funk that lasts two days and nothing I say makes it better, so I leave her alone. The next few days pass by very quickly and soon it's the Friday before the party.

Namrata walks into the office, looking haunted. I put down the pen in my hand and look at her in concern.

'What happened?' I ask her as she sits down, looking uncertainly at me.

'My brother and his wife are coming to the party tomorrow,' she says.

'Both of them?' I ask, surprised.

She nods. 'They don't really care if they embarrass me,' she says.

'Oh!' That doesn't sound good.

'I don't know what to do,' she says.

'Why did you even tell them about the party?'

'I had to. They wanted to know why I was going to the office on a Saturday,' she says, shaking her head.

I remain silent when all I want is to tell her how sad and pathetic it is that as an adult she's answerable to two people but she catches the look in my eyes and turns away.

'Is Farida coming to the party now that her plans have been cancelled?' she asks after a moment.

'I don't know. I haven't asked her.' The truth is, I'm torn between inviting Farida and Ajay.

'What about Mini? Who is she inviting?' she asks.

I shrug. I have no idea. Talk of the devil, and here she is. She pulls up a chair and sits down. 'So, you all set for tomorrow?' she asks Namrata, who looks up from her screen but doesn't say anything. Mini has told her about the plan to accompany her to class tomorrow and it's obviously made her anxious.

'I really don't think this is a good idea,' she says softly but seems to back away when Mini's face turns thunderous. Farida is best at putting Mini in her place and it's too bad she doesn't work with us.

'I won't make any trouble for you. I just need to speak to Akash alone. And I'll do it after class. I'll wait for you outside the building,' Mini says and stalks off.

Namrata looks at me, distressed, and I feel idiotic for having given the idea to Mini in the first place.

'Don't worry. It will be fine,' I tell her.

'I didn't want to go tomorrow but missing even a single class is not a good idea. There are only eight in all,' she says.

Later that evening, when it's almost time to leave, Vinay walks towards us and on seeing me, stops. Taking a deep breath, he starts walking our way again. I glance at Namrata.

She no longer freezes in his presence but she still avoids talking to him.

'Um, hi,' he says.

'What is it, Vinay?' I ask, while Namrata chooses to ignore him.

'May I . . . may I talk to Namrata in private?' he asks. Namrata tenses slightly at the mention of her name but doesn't look up.

'I'm busy,' she says.

This is even better than a movie. All that's missing is a tub of hot buttered popcorn. Vinay looks downcast but doesn't leave. He looks around nervously to see who has noticed because he's wary of office gossip.

Lowering his voice, he pulls up a chair and sits close to her. I move my chair further away even though I'm itching to know what he has to say. Namrata looks up at me, eyes round with panic but I stare back at her, trying to instil confidence.

'I think I'll get some coffee,' I say to no one in particular and get up. As I turn the corner to reach the coffee machine, I glance back to see Vinay talking to her earnestly. I can't see Namrata's face which is hidden by her monitor but I'm pretty sure her ears are red.

When I come back from my prolonged coffee break, I'm curious and excited. But *both* of them aren't there. What? I look around, almost in panic. Where could they have gone? Namrata is such a straight arrow, she wouldn't go anywhere without even asking for permission, let alone going home with Vinay. But apparently, that's what she's done. So much for the ice queen act. Humph! I'll have to wait till she reaches home to call her on the landline for the dishy details.

40

I forget all about Namrata and Vinay when I reach home because the unthinkable has happened. I unlock the door and let myself in and stop short because Farida is sitting on the sofa, talking to Irshad.

She looks up, her face glowing with happiness, and beams at me. Irshad gets up and shakes my hand. I suppose my bewilderment is easily discernible because he shakes his head and smiles.

'I'm sorry for dropping in unannounced but I knew something was wrong when she wasn't answering my calls for the past two days. Then yesterday she finally told me about her cancelled trip to Mumbai and I could sense her disappointment. So, I decided to come here instead,' he says, his voice low and dignified.

I smile because I don't know what to say.

'When did you get here?' I ask finally, when I spot the coffee table groaning under plates of sandwiches and brownies and tea.

'I reached Bangalore and called Farida,' he says, turning back to her with a smile. Great. So, in the two hours it must have taken him to reach the city from the airport, Farida has outdone herself in trying to prove the adage that the way to a man's heart is through his stomach.

'I'll just freshen up,' I tell him and stare meaningfully at Farida. She's supposed to understand that I want to talk to her and should make an excuse and follow me. Okay, so my non-verbal communication skills suck but she's my BFF and usually understands what I mean. Today, she looks back at me blankly.

I walk into my room and switch on the lights and then call out to her, wincing at how obvious it all seems. She comes in, looking irritated.

'What is it, Priya?' she asks.

'You couldn't call and tell me he's here?' I whisper.

'What difference does it make? It's all okay,' she says, crossing her arms.

'Look, you need to . . . you . . .' I'm lost for words. I don't know what to tell her. She makes a face, and walks out. At the door, she turns and mouths, 'I know what I'm doing.'

Great. Two of my friends think they know what they're doing when I know for a fact that they're both clueless when it comes to relationships. I take a quick shower and head back outside to see Farida and Irshad getting ready to leave.

'Where are you guys going?'

'Um, actually, Irshad wanted to go to the house,' Farida says, looking uncomfortable.

'I don't think it's a good idea,' I tell them. Farida looks caught between the chance to spend more time with Irshad and the dread of facing Reshma Phuppu and her husband.

'I don't know why you've let that impostor stay in your house for so long,' Irshad addresses Farida. 'Why didn't you complain to the police? Everything about that woman is shady.'

'I didn't know what to do!' she says. 'I was still in school when my parents died. She was there at home and it all seemed convenient at first.' Farida is twisting the edge of her dupatta. Today she's wearing a deep-maroon kurta paired with an egg-yolk-yellow churidar and dupatta. My eyes hurt.

'How could you just let them continue living there? Why didn't you kick them out when you came of age?' Irshad asks, unbuttoning the cuffs on his sleeves and rolling them up, right to his elbow. He does it all very casually but I can see Farida looking at him, eyes wide, like she has never seen a man do this before. Like he's doing something way more scandalous like removing his shirt.

'By then it was too late,' she says, turning away slightly. Irshad stretches his neck to ease the kinks.

'Let's go,' he says and, as though remembering me just then, asks me if I want to join them.

'No, but why do you want to go?' I persist.

He exhales loudly. 'She told me about not being able to find the house deeds,' he explains.

'There's no way I am letting her go back to that house after what that man did,' I tell him.

'Priya!' Farida looks at me shocked. She hasn't told Irshad anything about Reshma Phuppu's husband, I assume.

'It's okay. I already know what he did. I'm waiting to meet him,' Irshad says, cracking his knuckles menacingly. If he didn't look so serious, I'd laugh. This sophisticated, charming man who looks like he just stepped out of a gentlemen's club is all set to beat up Reshma Phuppu's husband.

Farida looks at both of us shocked. I avoid her gaze.

'How did you . . .' she trails off and then rounds on me. 'You! You can't keep your mouth shut, can you?'

I flinch. 'Look, I . . .'

She doesn't give me a chance to explain. 'You didn't have the right to tell him anything,' she says, her voice low and angry. Irshad turns to mollify her, but she silences him with a glare.

'Don't meddle in my business again, Priya,' she says firmly.

I'm taken aback as the harshness and weight of these words hit me. I'm her best friend. How can she say this to me? That too for Irshad. I feel self-righteous anger build up inside me.

'Oh please. If I hadn't told him, do you really think your one-sided pining would have brought him to our doorstep?'

I regret the words as soon as they leave my mouth. In the stunned silence that follows, I can feel my mouth go dry in panic. Farida has tears in her eyes but stares at me coldly, while Irshad looks at both of us like he can't believe what he's hearing.

'We're going. Don't bother to wait up,' Farida says and walks away, her tone chilly. Irshad looks thoroughly confused, but he shakes his head slightly and follows Farida. I walk after them, hoping to talk to Farida, to apologize to her, but she isn't waiting by the lift. She's taken the stairs and is already out of sight. Irshad sprints to keep up with her.

I call out to them to stop and wait for me when the lift arrives at our floor. Ignoring it, I'm almost at the steps when Natasha emerges from the lift, carrying a holdall. She looks dazzling as always, in an off-white silk shirt and blue jeans. She takes in my outfit in a disparaging glance and, lifting her head, walks towards Ajay's apartment, high heels clicking on the tiles. What is she doing here? Instead of ringing the doorbell, she pulls out a set of keys from her handbag, unlocks the door and enters.

41

I'm so dazed that I stand rooted to the spot for five whole minutes, wondering what Natasha is doing here. Ajay had told me he wasn't interested in her. And yet, here she was, dressed to kill. Probably dressed to seduce as well. I just wonder how she intends to do that with Anya around.

I shut my eyes briefly, remembered hurt flooding my mind when I recall how they looked like the perfect family. She's apparently not letting go without a good fight. I look down at my clothes and feel deflated instantly. My yoga pants are wrinkled and there's a chocolate stain on my top. I'm such a mess.

How would Ajay react to her presence? He had sounded sure that he wasn't interested in her and yet, here she was again. The Farida and Irshad drama completely forgotten, I quietly walk back to my apartment and sit down. Irshad's woodsy cologne still lingers in the air. It's too late to go looking for them now. They've probably reached the house already.

I'm mortified at what I did. Why did I have to blab like that? Now there's no one I can commiserate with. Farida is the one I turn to every time. Ajay is probably busy enjoying or fending off Natasha's attentions. Namrata would have been my ideal choice but she left with Vinay, so I have no other recourse but to call Mini.

'You won't believe where I'm going,' she says as soon as she answers the call. I realize she's put me on speakerphone.

'Where?' I ask, sitting up straight.

'I was on my way home when my phone rang. It was Vinay.'

Oh.

'I could barely understand what he was saying. He was babbling on about being locked in Namrata's house and the police being called. He wanted me to take her home with me,' she says.

What?

'What the hell? Why the police? Who's locked up?' Anxiety fills my stomach in a rush.

'I couldn't understand half of what he was saying.'

'Should I come too?' I ask, looking around for my scooter keys.

'It would be nice if you did. I don't know why they called me. I'm close to your place. I can pick you up,' she says.

'Fine,' I tell her and hang up. I change into a pair of jeans and a blue shirt and quickly step out, deciding to wait downstairs. I lock the apartment and send a quick text to Farida to tell her where I'm going. Two blue tick marks appear and she's online very briefly before disappearing. I know she's not going to reply.

I'm determined not to look at Ajay's door as I wait for the lift. Unfortunately, it opens as I wait and all three of them step out just as I shut the scissor gates. I look down at my feet as the lift takes me to the ground floor. I don't know where they're going and I can't bear to look at their perfect little family.

I'm at the gate of the apartment complex, waiting for Mini to show up, when Ajay's car glides up from the basement parking. He looks at me and waves, but I don't respond. Sitting next to him is Natasha who asks him something, making him turn towards her. I look away thankfully, spotting Mini's car.

I enter and strap myself in, not looking at her. She doesn't notice and continues the discussion from our call.

'What was Vinay doing with her? What's going on? Why do you guys leave out all the juicy gossip?' she asks.

From the corner of my eye, I can see Ajay's car cross the gate. I avoid looking in that direction and turn to Mini who is reversing.

I try to quickly update her about Namrata and even Farida. She takes her eyes off the road for a second and looks at me.

'Whoa! That is a lot of stuff for one day,' she says. I throw my head back and groan. I'm not looking forward to the party tomorrow. There's so much happening with everyone that it feels like I'm being pulled in ten different directions.

'Tell me about it,' I mutter, shutting my eyes briefly. In about five hours' time, I turn thirty. My best friend is mad at me, something weird is going on with my colleague, the guy I like is taking another woman out to dinner and my boss has been breathing down my neck to make sure *his* party is a success. Thirty already looks terrible.

42

Namrata's house is a nondescript two-storey building. Everything about it screams average. I can understand why she always seems so nervous and shy when someone asks her about her family and where she lives. What I don't understand is the commotion outside her house. There's a huge group of people hanging around, looking on with a great deal of interest. I try to make my way through the crowd while Mini parks.

'What's happening?' I mutter. When I reach the door, I spot Vinay arguing with two people. He turns to me and looks surprised, then relieved.

'You can ask her. This is Namrata's boss,' he says, turning to me. The man with whom he has been arguing is wearing a shirt that's two sizes too big. His clothes seem to hang off his body—like he's wearing borrowed clothes. But the clownish effect is marred when he crosses his arms and narrows his eyes and looks me up and down, derisively.

'This girl?' he asks. Ha. Girl is it? I turn thirty in a few hours. But now is not the time for useless vanity.

'I'm her boss. What's going on?' I ask, trying to infuse a sense of authority in my voice. 'Where's Namrata?'

Vinay turns to me and quickly explains what has happened. Vinay suggested he drop Namrata home. She'd wanted to wait for me but he'd hurried her and that's why she'd left. When they arrived though, Namrata's brother and his wife started making a huge scene about her coming home with a boy and locked her up and threatened Vinay.

'They've *locked* her up? Who the hell do they think they are?' I ask, my voice quivering in anger and disbelief.

'He's threatening to call the police,' Vinay adds. Mini joins us and she snaps when she hears the entire story.

'Where's Namrata?' she asks and I instinctively look up. She's at the window, her palms against the glass, looking troubled and scared.

'What the fuck? Who does this?' Mini almost roars in anger as she *ploughs* her way past Namrata's brother who momentarily looks taken aback and intimidated. She's fierce, my girl, I think with pride.

Instead of knocking him down, she turns to the swelling crowd and bellows at them to leave. Startled, they fall silent. One more bellow and she actually bends down as if to remove her shoe and they all scatter. I purse my lips to stop myself from laughing. With the crowd dispersed, Mini advances on Namrata's brother who now looks a little petrified. His wife, however, doesn't seem to be affected.

I glance at her, trying to remember what Mini had told me about her. Namrata's sister-in-law is wearing hot pink capris and a white sleeveless top, revealing long and bony arms. Her make-up looks sophisticated and her hair is pulled back in a high ponytail. If she'd been taller, much taller, she could have passed for a model. Namrata's brother seems embarrassed and proud of his wife at the same time. When she speaks, I understand why.

'Don't interfere in *avar* family business,' she says loudly, her voice like scratchy nails on a blackboard.

'Your family business? You've locked up my friend and we're not leaving until you let her go,' Mini says. An older woman is at the door, looking distressed. Her hair is steel grey and frayed and she's wringing her hands.

'*Ayyo devara!* This girl has brought such dishonour to my family,' she weeps.

'What dishonour?' Mini rounds on the woman and she cringes.

'She came home on a motorcycle with a strange man!' Namrata's brother exclaims, bristling at Mini's attitude.

'He's not a strange man. He's her colleague,' I reply, trying to maintain a calm demeanour although I'm getting angry as well.

'You can't lock up a grown woman for that,' Mini sneers. Before anyone can stop her, she barges in and runs upstairs. Vinay looks at me, clearly hassled.

'This is crazy,' he whispers.

Namrata's mother can only call out to her son, 'Raja, Raja', as he walks up to us menacingly, eyes popping in anger.

'You people need to leave. We don't want you here. I am going to call the police if you don't leave immediately,' he says.

'By all means call them,' Vinay says angrily. 'We'll tell them what you're doing.'

Where is Mini? Why hasn't she come down yet? Should I go up too?

'What are *we* doing? I said before, this is avar family matter,' Raja's wife cuts in angrily.

Before anyone can answer, we hear Mini clattering down the stairs followed by Namrata, who is carrying a suitcase. She looks down, refusing to meet anyone's eyes.

'What do you think you're doing?' Raja asks her furiously.

'What she should have done ages ago. She's moving out of this house,' Mini answers.

'You listen here. You can't do this. I'm calling the police,' Raja threatens. He looks at us nervously. His wife, however, stands in front of Namrata, feet apart, arms akimbo.

'Let's see how you leave with these people,' she taunts in a heavy accent. The disconnect between her accent and her language is jarring; it reminds me a little of Arvind. Mini looks at me as if to say, 'Can you believe this shit is for real?' and then takes Namrata's hand and firmly walks ahead.

'No one is going to stop us. And please call the police. Let's see what they'll do,' Mini tells her.

'Are you really going to go with *these* women?' Raja asks Namrata in Kannada, glaring at her. 'Have you thought about Amma even once? Is this how selfish you've become?'

'New haircut, new clothes, new boyfriend . . .' Raja's wife taunts, switching to Kannada too. Namrata's face floods with colour and I glance at Vinay, who looks uncomfortable even though he clearly doesn't understand what's being said.

'Who does she think she's fooling? Your mother should have got her married long ago,' the sister-in-law continues in Kannada. The mother in question looks at Namrata, almost sadly, and I feel a mix of anger and pity well up.

'Your sister is a slut,' she says, this time in English, looking up at us as though daring us to defy her words.

That does it! Both Mini and I move forward but Vinay has beaten us to it. However, before he can say anything in Namrata's defence, she steps forward.

'Stop it, bhabhi. You're embarrassing me in front of my friends. I've had enough,' she says quietly.

'You have the guts to talk to me this way?' the woman says in anger.

'Didn't the lady say she's had enough?' Mini intervenes. Vinay picks up Namrata's suitcase and Raja makes a move to stop him. There's an altercation and I look around to see the dispersed crowd slowly inching back.

'Stop it!' Namrata says, her voice too soft for them to take her seriously. She's distraught and I take her hand and move towards Mini's car.

'She's leaving!' Raja's wife yells and makes a lunge for us but Mini stops her and shoves her back.

'Yes, she's leaving with me. Let's see you stop us,' she says. Vinay brushes past Raja and picks up the suitcase.

'Let's go,' he says as we all walk towards the car quickly.

'I'm filing a police complaint!' Raja yells and shakes his fist in anger.

'Fuck off!' Mini yells back at him. Vinay grins and deposits Namrata's suitcase in the boot of Mini's car. He turns around and stops short. Namrata is staring at her house, tears rolling down her face as she opens the door and gets in. Her mother is at the door, shaking her head slowly. Raja and his wife go back inside and the old lady follows them, quietly shutting the door behind her.

Mini starts the car and I look at Namrata, wishing I knew the right words to ease her pain.

'On the bright side, your brother and his wife won't come for the party tomorrow,' I tell her. She doesn't even seem to hear me.

43

'Y ou're staying with me,' Mini announces once we're on our way. Vinay is following us on his bike.

Namrata doesn't say anything. She just nods and looks down, silently wiping away her tears.

Mini continues raving about psycho brothers and their neurotic wives who have no right to lock people up when they deserve to be in a mental institution themselves.

I check my phone to see if Farida has replied but she's still studiously ignoring me. I debate calling Irshad to find out how things are, but before I can follow through on that, Namrata starts talking.

'I don't know if I've done the right thing,' she says.

'What do you mean?' Mini asks incredulously. 'You actually want to live there?'

'No . . . I . . . I stayed with them for so long because of my mother. And today, she didn't even stand up for me when I had done nothing wrong,' she says. 'I just . . . I can't believe it.'

I don't know what to say to that.

'I feel like I've wasted all these years of my life,' she says, wiping away fresh tears.

There's an awkward silence. 'At least you're out now,' Mini says. Namrata looks a little lost when I turn in my seat to look at her.

'Tell me,' Mini begins, trying to catch Namrata's eye in the rear-view mirror, 'how come your brother's wife is so thin? And your brother, has he lost weight recently?'

Namrata sighs. 'He was quite plump and very fond of good food until he married Anita. She took over his diet and forced him to lose weight. She's obsessed with being thin.'

'She also talks a little funny,' I add.

Namrata nods, making a slight face. 'She has a big complex about that, actually. Both Raja and I studied in an English-medium school and our English is . . . not like hers. She gets annoyed whenever she hears me talk in English,' she says.

Wow. 'And it's okay for her to dress in Western clothes but not for you?' Mini asks the question that's been playing on my mind.

Namrata shrugs unhappily at the reminder of how she'd been so downtrodden in her own house.

'You know, I was thinking. Both of them being so skinny, do their bones clang together when they have sex?' Mini asks as she stops at a signal and turns to Namrata with a grin.

Poor Namrata turns red but then she actually smiles a little. I'm glad Mini has sensed Namrata's unease and is trying to lighten the atmosphere. But then, I say something that's been plaguing me all along.

'I still don't know what you were doing, going back home with Vinay.'

'I . . . he . . .' Namrata glances outside the window where we can see Vinay waiting beside us at the signal. He's looking ahead, unaware that we are looking at him. Then, as though sensing it, he turns his head. Pushing his helmet visor up, he shrugs, as though to ask what's wrong. For some reason, the question seems to be directed only towards Namrata, who shakes her head.

The signal changes and Mini zips ahead. There is not much traffic on this road for a change. She's going to drop me off first and then she'll take Namrata home.

'You still haven't answered me,' I remind her.

'He . . . he was sorry about the way he behaved with me before,' she says slowly.

'And?'

'And he wants another chance,' she whispers, looking down at her lap.

'Ooh! What did you say?' I ask.

'I was just so shocked. I told him I needed time,' she says finally.

'Good you didn't give in immediately,' Mini announces importantly.

I feel like scoffing at her because she'd told us that when she met Akash, she just knew there was no need to play games with him, that he was the one she was meant to be with. Then I remember the way she'd growled at the crowd and keep my thoughts to myself.

'He was actually surprised. He thought . . .' she trails away and shrugs.

'You'd say yes right away. Well good for you. You do need time to process these things,' I tell her as we finally come to a stop outside my apartment. Suddenly, I'm dreading going back inside. I don't want to see Ajay with Natasha and I don't know if Farida is back yet.

'Hey, isn't tomorrow your birthday?' Namrata asks as I get out and she comes around to sit in front.

I make a face and nod. 'Don't wish me in advance, okay? I need all my wishes on the day,' I tell both of them. Shaking her head, Mini drives off.

On my floor, I glance at Ajay's door, not sure if he's come back yet. I open the door to my apartment and once again, stop short. Farida is sitting stiffly on the single sofa with Irshad at her feet, his body turned towards her, his head on her lap. Er . . . what is happening here?

He looks at me and then straightens up, blushing. Farida still refuses to meet my eye.

'What happened?' I ask as he gets up and dusts the seat of his pants before sitting on the other sofa. He looks down at his hands and I note that his knuckles look bruised.

'Will someone tell me what's going on?' I screech.

They both look at me surprised. I've had enough. This whole day has been fucked up from the very beginning.

A knock on the door startles us all. Taking a deep breath, I open the door. Ajay is outside, but beyond him, I can see Natasha, looking at both of us with narrowed eyes.

'Not interested,' I tell him and shut the door in his stunned face.

'Priya . . .' I can hear him call out.

'Go away,' I tell him firmly and stride towards my room. I don't know if Farida is still mad at me but I'm bubbling with so much anger at everyone that I don't care.

44

'Here, have some of these,' Farida says, dropping a handful of Reese's Peanut Butter Cups in my lap. I unwrap one sullenly and start eating.

'Feeling better?' she asks. I don't reply.

'Look, you crazy woman, you really screwed up when you told Irshad about me pining for him. I didn't think I could ever forgive you for that,' she says.

'Then why the chocolates?' I ask her as I unwrap another and pop it in my mouth. The chocolate and peanut butter melt on my tongue and I finally feel a sense of calm.

'Irshad helped me find the house deeds. You won't believe where they were!' she says excitedly, as she sits down beside me. I'm all ears and I sit up straighter.

'Where?'

'My father had this weird hidey-hole in his study. I didn't even know it was there,' she says, her eyes shining. Wow! I wouldn't put it past her father to do something like that.

'How did you find out about it?'

'He'd shown it to Irshad when he'd visited us all those years ago. I don't even know how he remembered,' Farida continues.

'Some memory he has, huh?' I comment, unwrapping another chocolate. Trust Farida to know what I need. I'm feeling better already or maybe it's just the sugar rush and the fact that I haven't had dinner.

'Reshma Phuppu and her husband were very rude to us. But you should have seen their faces when Irshad found the deeds. He also punched her husband and broke his nose,' she says in a whisper.

'What?'

'I had no idea he was going to do that. Anyway, enough is enough. I have the property deeds with me and I can do what I want with that house. I kicked out Reshma Phuppu finally,' she says.

'You didn't!'

'I did too! And I did it on my own. I told her to pack up her stuff and get lost before I call the police,' she says.

'And that worked?'

'Well, having Irshad by my side and her husband's bleeding nose made her do it, I guess. She packed whatever she could and left, promising to get even. Irshad told her she'd have to deal with him.'

'Ooh!' I'm stunned at this turn of events.

'They don't know he's headed back to Mumbai soon,' she says, her voice lowering to a whisper.

'Now what? What was that scene I walked in on?' I look at her shrewdly.

She bites her lower lip and looks away, her eyes flooding with tears.

'Hey, what happened?' I ask softly.

'We came back here and he wanted to know about what you'd said. He . . . he wanted to know if it was true, if I loved him,' she whispers.

'What did you say?' I ask, feeling terrible for having blurted out her secret in front of him like that.

'Nothing. He could read my face. He knew it was true,' she whispers.

'And?'

'And nothing. He came and sat down like that, telling me how much I mean to him but . . .' she shrugs, her mouth quivering slightly.

We both stay silent. She looks up, wiping her eyes and sniffling a little.

'You drama queen. Why did you tell Ajay to get lost?' she asks.

'He took Natasha out for dinner. I can't deal with him if he can't make up his mind about her,' I tell her.

'Oh. I wish I'd known,' she says, looking guilty.

'Why?' I ask, suspiciously.

'Because I asked him to come in and introduced him to Irshad. He's sitting outside,' she says.

'My god, you're so meddlesome, Farida,' I snap at her. 'You think I messed up by telling Irshad about your feelings? Please. Maybe he'll ditch his fiancée and move to Bangalore to be with you.'

She snorts. 'Please. I've seen her photos on Facebook. She's stunning and a doctor too,' she says.

'Big deal. Now what am I going to do about Ajay?' I mutter.

'Talk to him? Please,' she says, nicking one of the chocolates and opening the wrapper.

'That's mine,' I growl.

'Go and talk,' she insists.

'But how can I with Irshad out there?'

She sighs.

'He's going to stay at the house tonight,' she says.

'Why? He can stay here, you know, in your room. You can sleep here, right?' I suggest.

'Yeah. You tell him that. I didn't want to say anything that would sound as though I don't want him to go,' she says.

'Fine,' I tell her and step out.

Ajay is on the sofa, talking to Irshad earnestly. He looks up when I walk in. Mom is right. His face does light up when he sees me. Steeling myself, I smile at Irshad and suggest that he sleep here tonight. He looks conflicted but then agrees after a while, saying they would need to change the locks in Farida's house before anyone can stay there.

I smile at him and then sit down on the sofa. Irshad looks around, ostensibly for Farida.

'She's in my room,' I tell him. His face flushes slightly and he nods.

'I think I'll go to sleep too. It's been a long day,' he says, getting up. His bag is near the door and he picks it up before going into Farida's empty bedroom.

I don't look at Ajay. The clock indicates that it's 11.45 p.m.

'It's late, Ajay. Can we talk later?' I say.

'Look at me, Priya,' he says. Childishly, I don't meet his eye.

'I swear I had no idea she was coming over this evening,' he says.

I exhale loudly. 'She has a key to your apartment. You take her out to dinner. You guys already look like a perfect family, and I think Anya also likes her a lot. I mean, why wouldn't she? She looks so much like your wife.'

'Anya hates her,' Ajay says, and I look at him in surprise. 'Why?'

'I don't know. They've never gotten along. Anya was so little when Kirti died but obviously she's seen pictures of her mother, and she hates that Natasha looks so much like her.'

'I still don't get it.'

'Who can understand what goes on in the mind of a five-year-old?' he muses. 'I think she reminds Anya of her mother but . . . she's not. Natasha is also mean to Anya most of the time. She's always snapping at her or not paying her any attention.'

I want to ask him how anyone can be mean to a five-year-old, but I don't.

'What are you doing here, Ajay?' I ask instead.

'I wanted to ask you out to dinner tomorrow. Just you and me. Anya is going to stay the weekend with Kirti's parents,' he says.

The possibilities seem endless but I'm not thrilled at the moment. 'And what about Natasha?' I ask him.

'She's going back tomorrow morning. She's taking Anya with her,' he says. I digest the information in silence. He leans forward, taking my hand, and speaks again. 'I know things have been unclear between us but I want to change that. I'm hoping you want that too. I want us to be together,' he says, leaning forward to hold my face in his hands but I back away. He looks surprised and hurt.

I shake my head. 'I have some questions for you tomorrow and then . . . maybe things can change,' I tell him. That's when I remember the party and my face falls.

'What's wrong?' he asks.

'I have an office party tomorrow. I don't know till when it will go on. I can't go to dinner with you,' I tell him.

The disappointment on his face is apparent as it's his only free night. Anya will be back on Sunday evening for school on Monday.

'I really don't know, Ajay. I've had one hell of a day and I want to sleep now,' I tell him. He nods and gets up to leave. I shut the door after him, still a little confused about my feelings.

I go back to my room and see that Farida is asleep on my side of the bed. She knows perfectly well that's my side.

I change my clothes, brush my teeth and get into bed when she turns over and looks at me.

'Happy birthday, you old woman,' she whispers.

'One day I'll return the compliment,' I promise her.

45

My day begins with a phone call from Arvind who wants to know if I've sent out the physical invites to all the stakeholders and whether I have a few extra. I have no idea what he's talking about until realization dawns and I wake up, groggily promising to get back to him when I reach the office.

'You aren't already in the office?' he asks, incredulously.

'Why? Are you?' I ask him, irritably. I squint and look at the clock on the wall. It's 7 a.m.

He's taken aback at my tone. 'Arvind, it's 7 a.m. The party is this *evening*,' I remind him through gritted teeth, forcing myself to be pleasant.

'But there are so many things to take care of—the sound system, catering, shamiana, chairs,' he goes on. I fall back on the bed and turn to see that Farida is missing.

'I've taken care of it all,' I tell him and end the call before he can continue. He's taken to micromanaging at a fine time, I fume.

There are lots of messages on my phone wishing me happy birthday but I scroll past them. No message from Ajay. Last night, when he'd asked me out to dinner, for a minute

I'd wondered if he knew it was my birthday. Apparently not. Well, can't blame a man for not being a mind reader, I think, as I get ready for what seems like the longest day of my life. Just as I'm dressed, my mother and brother call me in quick succession. They both end by telling me to enjoy the day. In my head I think it's a big ask.

Outside, Irshad and Farida are in the kitchen, drinking tea. There's an awkward silence between them and I get the feeling I may have interrupted a conversation.

'It's Priya's birthday today,' Farida says unnecessarily, pushing a mug of tea in my direction.

Irshad smiles. 'Happy birthday,' he says.

'Thanks,' I mutter.

'What happened with Ajay?' Farida asks. I glare at her. She could have asked me last night when I came to sleep but she'd started snoring immediately after wishing me. And now she wants me to relay what happened in front of Irshad?

'Nothing happened. Irshad, what are your plans for the day?' I ask, turning to him. Irshad glances at Farida and shrugs.

'We were thinking of changing the locks in the house,' he says.

Oh, 'We', huh?

Farida looks at the table, rubbing at an imaginary spot.

'We also need to discuss what to do with the house. I personally think she should sell it. Then she can do whatever she wants, right?' he addresses the question to me. Exactly what I've been telling her all along, I think.

'I can still do whatever I want,' she interrupts hotly. 'I have no intention of selling the house.'

Irshad seems taken aback by her vehemence. 'What will you do with the place? It's huge! There's so much maintenance involved, so much hard work,' he says.

'When people love something, they take care of it,' she replies. Are we still talking about the house, I wonder as my mobile buzzes with notifications.

'Why do you want to saddle yourself with a house? Sell it, be free! Buy an apartment in Mumbai; then I can keep an eye on you and not worry about you living alone here,' he says.

The silence in the room is actually palpable.

'You want me to move to Mumbai?' Farida asks, her voice low. I've known her long enough to know that when her voice reaches that decibel, it's a warning sign.

'Yes. I . . .' Irshad seems lost for words.

'And do what?' she asks.

'The same thing you do here. Paint, take photos.'

'What's the point of doing the same thing there? When I can do it here?' she asks.

'Because we'll be in close touch with each other,' he says, still baffled.

'And why would I want to be in close touch with you?'

'Because I care about you, Farida. Because you're family,' he says gently.

'I don't need you to care about me. I've managed pretty well on my own all these years. There is no way I'm selling the house and moving to Mumbai. If you care so much about me, why don't you sell your house and move here?' she asks.

Irshad is stunned into silence.

'Kids, kids, I have a lot of work to do today,' I say, trying to defuse the tension.

Both of them continue to stare at each other intensely. Sighing, I wash my mug and pick up my phone.

'Shut up and sit down, Priya. It's a Saturday and it's your birthday,' Farida snaps at me.

'Yes, but it's the annual office party tonight and Arvind called . . .'

'It's not even 8 a.m. The party is at night,' she says, standing up.

'What are you doing?' I ask, sitting back down again. She's right. I've taken care of everything. I don't need to go in until the afternoon, but I'm too wired to wait that long.

'Making breakfast,' she announces.

Irshad and I watch her in silence as she starts beating eggs for omelettes, asking us what kind we want. She's also making waffles. I look at her, focused on cooking, but intensely aware of the man in the kitchen, and I feel so much love towards her. That is, until the doorbell rings.

I groan. 'What have you done now?' I ask. Irshad looks amused.

'Let me get the door,' he says. I want to take the chance to quickly ask her how she feels about Irshad asking her to move to Mumbai, but before I can do that, he's already back, with Ajay and Anya. Great. Ajay's holding a plate with a dark chocolate cake and he beams at me.

'Birthdays should begin with cake, right?' he says, setting it down on the table. I couldn't agree more.

46

When I finally arrive at the office, I feel some of the sugar rush of the morning dissipate as I hunt down the physical invites and send one of the office boys to Arvind's home with them. Ajay's chocolate ganache cake was absolutely delicious, and I wonder what time he woke up to bake *and* frost it.

Most of the work is done but I still have to supervise and ensure that everything works perfectly. I'm waiting for Namrata to join me after her creative writing class and I hope that having her around will take some of the burden off my shoulders. Just then Amrita walks into the conference room that I've set up as my temporary office for the event.

Ugh! I'd forgotten that she was coming back. Arvind had conveniently not told me when she was starting work again.

'What are you doing here?' I ask her as I look up from the list of people who will be winning various performance-related awards this evening.

'I've been asked to help,' she says sulkily. 'What do you need me to do?'

'Hang on,' I tell her, looking at the time on my phone. Namrata should be joining us soon. And right on cue, Namrata walks in with Mini, who looks thunderous.

'What happened?' I ask both of them, barely registering Amrita's shocked face when she sees how beautiful Namrata looks.

'Nothing happened,' Mini says, sitting down on one of the chairs with a thump. 'Why isn't it evening already? I need a drink. Are you going to the party in those clothes? Oh, happy birthday, by the way.'

'Thanks. No, I've brought along a change of clothes for the evening. I hope you guys have something else too?'

Namrata nods and I can sense that she's unhappy. Is it because of Amrita's presence? But she's barely noticed her. Amrita is still looking a bit gobsmacked because when she'd left, Namrata did not look like this and Mini wasn't on such good terms with us. Her expression becomes almost comical when Mini mentions something about Namrata staying with her.

'Namrata *lives* with you?' she asks in an awed whisper.

'You've got a problem with that?' Mini snaps at her and she shrinks.

'No, I . . . sorry,' she blabbers and turns to me. 'You were going to give me some work?'

'Yeah. Namrata is making the table arrangements for dinner this evening. She's worked out the seating arrangement as well. Just go with her and do whatever she tells you to do,' I say, enjoying the look of consternation on her face. I remember how she and Ayaz used to make Namrata toil while they frittered their time away.

Namrata is too decent a person to even think of things like revenge and comeuppance. She smiles briefly at Amrita and thankfully does not revert to her timid ways. Instead, she gives a list to Amrita and asks her to check the name cards on the tables and call the catering company to confirm the number of servers.

Stunned, Amrita heads upstairs. I feel pumped, but Namrata still looks troubled.

'What's the matter?' I ask her. She indicates with her eyes that she wants to talk to me in private. Both of us look at Mini, who is doodling aimlessly on a scrap of paper.

Trying not to make it look too obvious, both of us leave the conference room together and Namrata catches hold of my arm.

'What is it?' I ask her, surprised.

'Mini came with me to the class today. She wanted to talk to Akash but he wasn't there. In fact, he didn't come at all. Someone else took his class. So she left angrily and went to wait for me in the car. As I was leaving, I asked the receptionist about Akash and she said that his wife had an ultrasound appointment today, which was why he hadn't come in.'

I clap my hands over my mouth. Akash's wife is pregnant!

'She's *five* months pregnant,' Namrata adds. I do the math. If she's five months pregnant and Akash had been with Mini for three months before breaking up with her last month, then he'd lied to her about planning to leave his wife. He entered into a relationship with Mini, knowing fully well that his wife was pregnant. The lying creep.

'I take it you haven't told Mini?' I ask Namrata.

Her face blanches and she shakes her head. 'No. I'm too scared,' she whispers.

'We'll do it together on Monday then,' I tell her. She nods and then shyly pulls out a gift-wrapped parcel from her handbag.

'What's this?' I ask, touched and surprised.

'Nothing much. You know I don't have much money. It's just something I had with me, something I took with me when I left my house last night,' she says. 'Happy birthday. I hope you enjoy it.'

Intrigued, I open the present. It's a copy of *The Great Gatsby*. I smile at her, touched.

'Your favourite?' I ask. She nods.

'Have you read it?' she asks. I nod. Of course.

'Oh no, I should have got you something else then. I'm so foolish,' she says and I shake my head.

'No, please. It's perfect. It's one of my favourites too,' I tell her. 'And it means a lot to me that you gave me something you love.'

We go back to the conference room where Mini is on her phone.

'Did she tell you what Vinay said to her last night as he was leaving my house?' Mini asks, looking up. I turn to Namrata, who has turned beetroot red.

'What? No! What did he say?'

'There's something wrong with him,' Namrata mutters, tucking a strand of hair behind her ear. She's still quite red-faced.

'What did he say? What's wrong with him?' I ask, looking from Mini to Namrata, feeling irritated.

'I told her that I love her.'

We all look up, shocked to see Vinay standing at the door of the conference room, eyes ablaze with intensity and focused only on Namrata.

'And there is nothing wrong with me. I meant what I said,' he says, stepping inside.

My god. These two could teach Bollywood a lesson about drama.

47

Vinay looks at us pointedly, expecting us to get up and leave. Ha. Not happening. Miss out on this? No way! I share a look with Mini, who grins. We bloody made this happen. We're jolly well going to see how it plays out.

To my amusement, Amrita who has just come down for a break, looks like she's about faint. She's obviously heard Vinay's declaration.

'What all have I missed since I left?' she murmurs as Vinay frowns a little and indicates with a tilt of his head that he wishes to speak to Namrata in private. For once, Namrata understands immediately and shakes her head.

'You can talk here. In front of them,' she says.

I turn to Amrita who is waiting to hear what Vinay has to say. 'Loads of work to do, Amrita. Chop-chop,' I tell her briskly. I feel almost sorry for the kid until I remember how obnoxious she'd been to me and Namrata.

'But . . .'

'Go upstairs and we'll join you in a bit,' I tell her. Pouting, she leaves.

'Okay, everyone sit down,' Vinay says. 'You guys are making me nervous.'

He pulls up a chair for Namrata and sits facing her.

'I know what I said yesterday might seem a bit sudden to you,' he starts. Mini snorts loudly and Vinay turns to her, annoyed. I shush her, wishing there was popcorn.

'But I mean it with all my heart.'

Namrata is shaking her head slowly. 'You didn't even know I worked here until a little while ago,' she says softly.

'I'm an idiot,' he says sheepishly.

'I still don't understand why you would proclaim your love for me,' she says. 'You don't know me at all. And I'm older than you. I thought you had a problem with that.'

Mini and I share a look again, feeling proud of Namrata. I mean, this is Vinay, the office hottie who anyone would be happy to even have a fling with, and Namrata is giving him a hard time.

'That took a little bit of mental adjustment. I mean, I never would have guessed in a million years that you are older than me,' he says, leaning forward to take her hand. She pulls it away and takes a deep breath.

'Vinay, I'm just embarrassed by the whole thing. When we went for lunch, you didn't talk to me at all. And now you say you love me. How did that happen?'

Vinay looks at us, a little overwhelmed. He's probably never tried so hard for anything in his life. I shoot him a sympathetic look.

'I know I behaved like an ass. An old school friend called to catch up with me and I just hung on to that call like a lifeline because I was still figuring everything out. I was also very nervous. And even though I didn't speak to you at lunch, I couldn't stop thinking about you after that.

'It seemed like an alternate universe had opened up, one where we already knew each other, where we were friends and even more. And after last night, I just knew it and I had to say it to you.'

There's silence in the wake of his speech. But Namrata is not going to give in easily.

'It means something to me, you know,' Namrata says. 'Don't fling around words just for fun. I don't think it's funny.'

Vinay's face actually turns a little pink. 'I'm not flinging words around!' he protests.

'We've never even spoken properly until yesterday when you said you wanted another chance with me. Then you came home and all that stuff happened. How could you have fallen in love with me between then and the time it took to reach Mini's house?'

Let's say my jaw just hit the floor. Go Namrata!

Vinay stands up and runs his hand through his hair, frustrated. He paces before her and stops.

'You've been on my mind since the time the other intern told me you were in love with me,' he says finally. Uh oh. Namrata's face pales.

'She said what?'

'Mini, um, let's check on things upstairs,' I tell her and get up, but Namrata pins me down with a glare.

'What is he talking about?' she asks me. 'You knew? Is that why you did all this? Out of pity for me? I thought we were friends.' Her voice breaks slightly.

Shit! Shit!

'It's not like that,' I quickly intervene. 'I just thought it would help you with your confidence. That's all.'

Namrata looks from me to Vinay, standing up. 'I don't know what to think any more,' she says softly.

'Don't think. Just feel,' Vinay urges her, taking her hand and placing it over his chest dramatically.

'Oh, shut up!' Namrata tells him as she pulls her hand away. This time, Mini's jaw drops to the floor.

'You're nothing but a kid who suddenly finds me attractive because of these clothes and my hairstyle. I had a crush on you and you *crushed* me when we went on that date where you didn't talk to me. I don't think I want to attend this party. I'm going home,' she says suddenly and then stops, her hand over her mouth.

'I don't even have a home.'

'Nonsense. My house is your house,' Mini tells her briskly. I didn't imagine this would happen when Vinay talked to Namrata. I so didn't imagine this.

Vinay looks shocked.

'Look, I was an idiot,' he starts. Namrata doesn't seem to be listening to him. He takes her hand again and this time because she's lost in her thoughts, she lets him.

'I swear I wasn't even looking for a relationship after my last break-up,' he says. 'But you don't get to tell me how I do or do not feel.'

'Okay, fine. So, you love me. What should I do about that?' Namrata asks. I stare at her, amazed. I'd never have dreamt that Namrata would speak this way, to Vinay of all people.

Vinay looks stumped too. 'Give me a chance to prove it to you,' he says quickly. 'Let's go for lunch now. I want to get to know everything about you.'

Namrata looks at us. 'Might as well,' she says. 'I'm hungry.'

With that, she leaves the conference room, sweeping out, with Vinay following her. Mini claps slowly and turns to me.

'Best movie ever,' she whispers.

'Shh!' I tell her. I'm not saying I'm intimidated by Namrata, but I really don't want another friend angry with me.

48

Soon, some of the other volunteers join us upstairs and, with a lot of elbow grease, we're able to convert the terrace into a lovely-ish venue for the party. Arvind keeps calling to run his speech by me.

'I didn't know you were a jack of all trades,' Mini remarks as we finally sit down on the plastic chairs. We need to get ready soon. Namrata hasn't yet returned with Vinay.

'Arvind wants me to check whether this phrase is witty enough, whether people will get his sarcasm or not,' I can't help rolling my eyes as I tell Mini, who looks back at me steadily before bursting out in laughter.

'Sarcasm? Oh my god, you're not serious, are you?' she says, as she keeps laughing.

'What he said,' I mutter with a slight grin. I'm hungry too. We haven't had lunch yet, although in the morning I felt like I couldn't possibly eat for a month after that scrumptious breakfast.

As though reading my mind, Mini gets up. 'Let's go downstairs and order some food. I'm hungry.' I call out to

Amrita to join us and she looks almost surprised that we want to feed her.

On our way downstairs, I tell Mini about what happened with Farida and Irshad, and she's all ears.

'There is really way too much drama in our lives,' she says. Amrita who has been listening in as well, is wide-eyed.

Namrata and Vinay are not back yet, and I wonder what's happening with them.

'I hope they're coming back for the party,' Mini says. Amrita continues to remain baffled. She would have probably thought she was hallucinating if she'd seen how Namrata had decimated Vinay.

'Call them,' Mini says. I pull out my phone reluctantly and dial Vinay's number, putting the call on speakerphone because Mini is crowding me, wanting to listen in.

'Hey,' Vinay's voice crackles.

'When are you guys coming back? Get food for us too,' Mini says.

'Huh? What?'

'Food, dude. Food. Bring some for us as well,' she repeats.

'Okay, okay,' he says and ends the call. It's certainly not the quiet lunch Vinay had hoped to have with Namrata because Mini keeps calling him with updated food orders for the three of us.

While we wait, Mini starts telling me about her failed attempt to meet Akash today. I feel uncomfortable listening to her. Should I tell her the truth? But she'll be mad and I don't want her to run off alone to confront him. I can't leave the party to go with her. So, I listen in silence.

Mini notes that I'm not responding to her story but she doesn't say anything.

'What did Ajay get you for your birthday?' she asks finally.

'It's your birthday today?' Amrita interrupts. I nod and then turn to Mini.

'Well, he was at home last night but he didn't know it was my birthday. I think Farida told him early this morning, because he came over with Anya with a lovely chocolate cake. Yummy ganache frosting and all!'

'Whoa! He baked the cake?' Mini asks. She then turns to Amrita. 'Ajay is her neighbour who has the hots for her. He's this lovely guy with a daughter and he's been pursuing Priya for quite some time now. He bakes and everything. And he's quite the hottie as well!'

Amrita blinks.

'Wow,' she mutters. I roll my eyes, feeling secretly pleased. 'How old *are* you?' she asks and my face falls slightly.

'Thirty,' I tell her, feeling the word in my mouth, its weight now a reality for me. It doesn't feel that dreadful now. More like full. My life feels fuller now, with all my friends, their lives, their loves and, of course, Ajay. I smile.

'I thought it would suck to turn thirty,' Amrita says faintly. I turn to her.

'I thought that too,' I tell her.

'And now you don't?' she seems genuinely curious.

'Doesn't really make much of a difference, to be honest.' It's the truth. Mini is looking at me speculatively.

'I'm turning thirty too next month,' she says.

Amrita turns to her, shocked. 'But . . . you . . . I thought . . .'

'Yeah, I know, I look much younger. And it's not like I'm ridiculously pleased about that, like Priya here.'

'Ha ha, very funny,' I tell her.

She ignores me. 'It's just genetic, I think. My dad is sixty but he looks forty-five. And here comes the next almost thirty-year-old,' she announces as Namrata walks in with Vinay, who is holding a massive bag of food.

'Why did I just spend so much money on food for all of you?' he grunts as he places the bag on the conference table and dusts his hands.

'You're treating us because if it weren't for us, you wouldn't have found the love of your life,' Mini says. Namrata shushes her, but she's smiling. Whew! This could mean that Vinay has charmed her enough to listen to him. But she doesn't look at me, so I don't know how angry she is with me.

'You just want free food, Mini. Admit it.' He laughs as he settles down in a chair and tugs Namrata's hand so she sits next to him. Well, that lunch worked wonders then.

'I think I want to turn thirty too,' Amrita whispers as she tears open the packaging on her burger and starts eating, her eyes on Vinay and Namrata as though she can't believe what she's seeing.

49

My phone rings just as I emerge from the restroom after changing for the evening. Mini isn't planning on changing and I don't know whether Amrita has brought a change of clothes. But Namrata goes in after I come out and I mentally give a thumbs up to her choice for today. She's got a simple flowy Anarkali suit that is not too grandiose or blingy but fits her perfectly. It has a pattern of pretty flowers and is sleeveless.

I make a face when I realize my phone is still ringing. It's probably Arvind trying to find out for the last time if his speech is 'abzolutely fine' or 'fantabulistic'. Ugh!

It's Farida.

'Irshad is leaving,' she says bluntly. Oh.

'I'm sorry,' I tell her with a sigh and head upstairs, the phone wedged between my neck and shoulder. 'Listen, it's probably for the best.'

'What do you mean it's for the best?'

'He has a life back there, Farida. He obviously has to go,' I explain.

'I know that. It's just . . . just that . . . you should have let things be. Why did you have to go and tell him about my feelings?' she asks.

'Did he say something?'

I pass one of the volunteers on the way and he looks at me appreciatively and grins. 'Looking good!' he says and I grin at him even though I'm sad for my friend on the phone who is just a few sentences away from breaking down into tears.

I took a good look at myself in the mirror before leaving the restroom. I've chosen this wine-coloured knee-length dress that fits me beautifully. It's slightly shimmery and has ruffles near the hem that rise and fall as I walk. I've left my long wavy hair loose and not done too much to it. On the terrace, everything is set up and people are trickling in. The caterers have set up the buffet stations and I go over to the tables in the front which are reserved for the big guys, the stakeholders and investors, and other VIPs Arvind wants to impress tonight.

I check the name cards, indicate to the sound guys to start the music and take a deep breath. Everything looks good so far. Farida is still on the phone with me and I need to let her go.

'No,' she says. 'But I'm so embarrassed about the whole thing now.' I wince, feeling a little guilty about the situation, but I need to make her see reason.

'Listen, why are you spending the few minutes of his time here talking on the phone with me? You're sitting in the loo, right?'

'If you hadn't said anything, he would have at least visited me again,' she sniffles. 'Now he just wants to leave and never come back.'

'How do you know that? Have you asked him?' I look around, my eyes widening in appreciation when I spot Namrata. She looks very pretty, and I see many heads turn as she walks up to me.

'No, but I don't need to. I know he won't,' she insists.

'Farida, I'm sorry, I'll have to talk to you later. I'm sure everything will be okay. Just talk to him,' I tell her and end the call.

'Listen . . .' I tell Namrata uncomfortably.

'No, you listen,' she says. 'I'm sorry for getting angry with you. You were just trying to help me.'

'I didn't do it out of pity,' I tell her although it's not entirely true. I'd also wanted to make her feel better about herself.

She shakes her head and smiles. 'I know. I have changed quite a bit being around you guys. And now that I'm staying with Mini . . .' she trails off.

I exhale loudly. 'Well, what did Vinay say? You seemed all right when you returned. Was it just the hunger talking?'

Clearly, some of Amrita's eye-rolling has rubbed off on Namrata too. She rolls her eyes with practised ease. 'He's like this adorable puppy and . . .' she breaks off. 'What?' she asks when she sees my mouth agape.

'Who *are* you?' I ask her uneasily.

'Why?' she asks baffled.

'That puppy analogy is something Mini or I would make.'

She shrugs. 'It was you guys who put that thought in my head. Remember? When we were watching that TV show?'

I scrunch up my forehead, trying to think. 'Which one?'

'That guy in the skirt? Vinay reminds me of him sometimes,' she says.

I burst out laughing. Jamie from *Outlander*. And, ahem, that was a kilt and not a skirt. Namrata was caught up in the story until Jamie and Claire began to have sex. I swear her eyes fell out then. She turned to us, eyes wide and shocked, mouth open. Mini plans to make her watch *Spartacus* next. She has no idea what's in store for her.

'Jamie is not like a puppy. He's a hulking man. But yeah, he's also very adorable,' I tell her.

'Haan, same thing,' she also grins.

'Stick with us, kid,' I tell her, trying to control my laughter.

'I'm quite fond of puppies actually,' she says with a grin.

Before I can reply, I realize that Arvind is here. He's looking around importantly, dressed in a three-piece suit. He spots me and starts walking my way.

'Everything is happening too soon,' Namrata continues. 'This is the first time I'm staying away from my family. I still need to understand what I want and . . .' she stops, probably thinking about her mother.

'You did the right thing with your family,' I tell her quickly and try to escape but Arvind has already spotted me.

'Priya!'

'Your speech is perfect and you're looking very dapper today,' I tell him before he can ask me to listen to his speech again.

He looks taken aback. 'Really?' he asks, pleased.

'Yes, I've got to . . .'

'No wait. I wanted to tell you that one of the team leads from Brightway's US team has recently quit her job and I heard that she's looking for a job in Bangalore and I want her to work with us. I'll be pitching to her during dinner and I want to make sure . . .'

I stop listening to him because I've realized Namrata has stiffened. She looks anxious and worried.

'. . . that we give her the right impression tonight. She's got a lot of experience and if we get her on our list of—oh, here she comes,' he says, straightening up as a beautiful woman walks over to us. She's dressed in black and her face is slightly full, but everyone can see why she's glowing. She's pregnant and smiling up at the man next to her, who's holding her hand.

'Hello, hello! Welcome to Citron,' Arvind bleats as she shakes his hand. Arvind is so taken by her that he almost bows. The man with her looks bored and then suddenly seems to recognize Namrata.

'Don't I know you from class?' he asks. I feel my stomach sink. Uh oh! No. This can't be happening.

'Hi, Akash,' Namrata says weakly. I turn to her, my lips pursed and she looks at me helplessly. Where is Mini? What will she do if she sees him?

'Fancy seeing you here,' he comments and puts his arm around his wife's shoulder, rubbing her arm. No one would ever guess that this loving husband had left poor Mini heartbroken last month.

Arvind leads them away and Namrata and I wonder how we can prevent the disaster that seems inevitable. Mini is on the other side of the terrace, at the open bar, happily getting drunk. I'm not sure there is any way we can salvage this evening.

50

At around 8 p.m., Arvind taps the mike and starts speaking. I use the opportunity to slip away. Namrata, who has been standing somewhere on the sidelines, follows me. We have to get Mini away from here. She wanted closure, but not here, not like this.

I feel frustration mount as I can't spot Mini. Where is she?

'Can you see her?' I ask Namrata, who shakes her head. We scan the crowd and finally spot her at one of the corner tables at the back, where she's sitting, quietly sipping her drink and checking her phone. Then I see that her earphones are in. Whew!

I tap her shoulder gently and she looks up, a little startled, and then smiles. 'Hey!' She takes out the earphones and wraps the cord around her phone.

'Want to go home?' I ask her. She frowns. 'But we haven't even had dinner yet!'

'Who cares! Poor Farida has been moping around because Irshad is going back to Mumbai. Come, let's cheer her up. We'll pick up some food on the way,' I tell her, sitting on my haunches beside her. Ouch. This is a bloody painful position in my heels. Namrata is standing right opposite her and we're trying to block her view of the tables in the front.

'Don't you need to be here and organize all the cabs and shit?' she asks slowly.

'Don't worry about it. I'll put Amrita on the job,' I improvise.

'Okay, let's go then,' she says, slurring the slightest bit. Feeling inordinately relieved, I get up, my knees wobbling painfully, and grab her arm. Of course, Arvind has to stop speaking just then. There's a short lull and then he begins to drone on again.

'We're very happy to have one of our most esteemed clients with us here today,' he says.

'Let's go, let's go,' I tell Mini, urging her to get up.

'Quite a few of you would have worked with her on the Brightway project,' he continues.

'Whoa! She's here? Bitch client from hell?' Mini says, blinking. 'I've got to see how many heads she has.'

Aargh! 'You've worked with her?' I ask, my voice rising slightly.

'Yeah. She made my life hell, especially when she joined the US team. What is she doing here?' Mini frowns. Her words are slurring even though she looks rather lucid.

'We're so pleased to inform you all that Ms Hrishita has agreed to join Citron as one of the lead project managers,' he announces.

'What?' Mini gasps loudly. She turns to me, her eyes wide.

'Come let's go,' I urge her but she shakes off my hand and I look at Namrata in dismay. This is bad. There is polite applause at Arvind's words. The others who have worked with Hrishita are all shell-shocked too.

'This can't be happening,' Mini whispers as she slides back into her seat. 'I can't work with her, man.' I sit down opposite her and motion to Namrata to stand strategically so Mini won't be able to see the stage.

'I invite her now to say a few words,' Arvind says and I groan. Mini looks around Namrata, irritated that she's blocking her view and motions her to move aside, but Namrata turns around, pretending not to have heard.

Hrishita takes the mike and starts addressing the crowd. Her voice is firm and husky, and she sounds extremely straightforward. She does not gush like Arvind. Instead she tells us that she hopes to take Citron to new levels and is happy for the opportunity. But then she starts talking about personal stuff and I shut my eyes in despair.

'As you can all see, we're expecting a new arrival in the family,' she says with a smile and the audience titters politely. 'Of course, it was completely unexpected. My husband, Akash, and I thought we had plenty of time but I think deep down I wanted this. I wanted to be with him, support him in his creative writing venture and have my baby here among family and the people I love. The offer from Citron was so serendipitous. Thank you so much!'

The applause is louder and then she hands the microphone back to Arvind who starts gabbing about new horizons and new opportunities and other shit. I try to pretend that nothing has happened as I tug at Mini's arm.

'Come, let's go!' I tell her but she pulls my hand away and turns to face me. She's breathing heavily.

'That's Akash's wife, isn't it?' she asks. I try to stall her but she stops me, shaking her head.

'You knew and that's why you were trying to make me leave,' she states.

I feel heat rush to my face. 'Don't worry. I won't make a scene,' she says, getting up from the table and swaying a bit. She clutches the table for support and then straightens up.

'What are you doing?' I follow her, worried and anxious. I don't care about the embarrassment the scene might cause Arvind, but I'm afraid for her and how devastated she's going to feel. She weaves her way to the front, with Namrata and I following her.

Dinner hasn't begun yet but I can see the servers getting ready. Mini has already reached the front and is facing Akash, who looks shocked to see her. Arvind looks at her in surprise.

'Hrishita, you may have worked with Mini, of course,' he says finally. 'She is one of our most talented software engineers.'

Hrishita cocks her head and smiles, her hand splayed on her belly in a contented manner. 'Hi! I've been looking forward to meeting you,' she says with a smile. Mini seems almost baffled. Hrishita beckons Mini to sit down beside her which confuses Mini even further, but she follows. She avoids Akash, who looks like he'd rather be anywhere but here.

Hrishita takes a deep breath. 'I wanted to meet you in person. I can be a pretty demanding client and many colleagues have told me that my emails are brusque and often not tactful. I'll be working with you again and I don't want you to have any hard feelings over whatever horrible inputs

I've given you so far,' she says. Hrishita sounds like a decent person. I glance at Akash, who looks very uncomfortable.

Mini nods. 'Sure,' she says, her voice breaking slightly. What is she going to do? Will she tell Hrishita about her and Akash? She gets up a bit unsteadily and clutches my hand.

'Let's go,' she whispers and doesn't turn to look at Akash, who appears relieved. I feel affronted on her behalf. Why does he get the easy way out?

'Actually, wait,' I tell Mini and hold her hand.

'No, no, please,' she whispers.

Namrata, who is standing with me, suddenly speaks. 'Congratulations on your baby, Hrishita. Akash is a lucky man. But he's not a very good man,' she says. Akash looks at her, furious.

'What?' Hrishita is obviously amused. 'How do you know him?'

'I'm a student in his class. Mini too has attended his classes,' Namrata speaks quietly.

'Oh,' Hrishita lets that sink in, her amusement vanishing, but then she smiles. 'That's a nice coincidence.'

'It is,' I add. 'And Namrata is right. He's not a good man.'

Hrishita's face takes on a puzzled look. 'Look, I'm hoping to join this company and do something good here. Is there something I should know?'

'You don't have to worry about me. I quit,' Mini says quietly. I swivel my head towards her, stunned. What?

'Let's go,' she urges us both. Namrata and I follow her quietly. I turn back once to see Akash looking stricken and Hrishita gazing at her distended belly, stroking it thoughtfully.

51

'You can't possibly quit!' I tell Mini as we head downstairs, Namrata following us. She keeps looking around to see if Vinay is around, I suppose.

'I can't possibly work with her,' Mini says quietly, heading off towards her desk. I've never really been to her work area before. The partition wall that doubles up as a whiteboard has several scrawls in her unintelligible writing. There are a couple of plants by her computer but everything else seems clean until she slides open the drawers, which are crammed with things.

'You don't have to do this *now*,' I tell her, sitting down beside her.

'Are you helping me or not?' she asks, rubbing her face and then her eyes. 'This is like a bloody nightmare.'

I run to the pantry, find a cardboard box for her belongings and bring it back. Namrata is already helping her sort some of her things into piles. Mini clutches her head.

'My head is spinning,' she mutters as she starts dumping things into the cardboard box.

'Don't rush into this. Think about what you're doing,' I tell her. Namrata shares a quick look with me, shaking her head slightly.

'Put yourself in my position, okay?' Mini erupts suddenly. 'Do you think you'd be able to work for the woman who is married to the man you were in love with? When she's having his baby?' she swallows. She scrunches her forehead and hits it with her curled fist lightly.

'I'm such an idiot,' she chants. 'You guys were right.'

'Listen,' I try to reason with her but she puts her hand up to stop me.

'Fucking stop, okay? I have to do this. I can't work for her. No way,' she continues dumping her things into the box. Her voice quivers as she switches on her computer. Namrata helpfully offers her a pen drive to save all her personal files which she does with remarkable alacrity.

'What will you do? Don't you need a job?' I ask her.

'I do. I'll figure something out. Maybe I'll take my dad up on his offer and visit him. Maybe . . . I don't know,' she says and stiffens. What? I turn around and see Hrishita walking up to us, head held high.

'Mini, I want to talk to you,' she says and pulls up a chair. Mini shakes her head.

'I don't. I really don't want to talk to you,' she says, continuing with her work.

'Listen. I can't imagine how you must feel but . . .' She breaks off when Mini turns to her, her eyes blazing.

'You can't. You're married to him, having his baby and, until last month, he was promising me that he was going to leave you,' Mini says, swallowing loudly. To our surprise, Hrishita's face remains placid and calm.

'He's done it before, hasn't he?' I ask suddenly. She turns to me and nods. She sighs loudly.

'I don't know why I thought he'd changed. I'd stopped taking on-site assignments because of him, but then I couldn't pass on such a huge project. I should have known he wouldn't have stayed faithful,' she says.

Mini stares at her.

'Then I found out I was pregnant. Right after I reached the US. I couldn't come back immediately so I stuck around for the first trimester and left only when the doctors said it was okay to travel,' she says.

'So what should *I* do?' Mini mumbles, still moving her mouse restlessly.

'I'm leaving him,' Hrishita announces. We all look at her shocked.

'He's vain and egotistical. He doesn't deserve me or someone like you,' she says with a shrug.

Mini is silent as she processes the words. Hrishita reaches out and places her hand on Mini's.

'I just feel like such a fool,' Mini whispers finally, looking up.

'Imagine how I feel,' Hrishita says almost wryly. 'I'm going upstairs to tell him I'm leaving. Leaving him. I told him I needed the restroom and came here hoping I'd find you. Do you want to join me?' she addresses the question to all of us.

Mini looks conflicted. But before I can say anything, my phone starts ringing. It's Farida again. I almost ignore her call but, knowing she's probably feeling low because Irshad is leaving, I move away a bit as I answer. She's talking so fast I can't understand a word of what she is saying.

'Slow down, slow down,' I tell her, feeling my stomach fall weightlessly and my breath become shallow.

'I can't!' she screeches and babbles until her phone is taken away and I hear Ajay's voice come on the line. There's a sense of urgency to his voice and yet it calms me.

'Priya, Irshad has been attacked by Farida's aunt's husband and some of his men.'

'What?' I collapse on a chair, unable to believe what I'm hearing.

'They were waiting for him outside the apartment and the moment he left, they attacked him. Thankfully, I was leaving in my car. I got out and chased them away. I called Farida and we're taking him to the hospital right now. There's a lot of blood, and it looks pretty bad,' he says, handing over the phone to Farida.

'Farida, listen, calm down. He'll be fine,' I tell her, trying to make my voice as soothing as possible but it's so difficult, especially since I'm freaking out.

'He's unconscious, Priya! He can't die!' she screeches.

52

I calm Farida down enough to make her tell me the name of the hospital. It's easily an hour's distance from here. Everyone looks at me expectantly and anxiously and I quickly tell them what has happened.

'Take my car and go,' Hrishita offers. I shake my head.

'No, I'll take an Uber or something,' I tell her but she holds my hand.

'My driver will get you there faster. It's really no problem,' she insists. I know it would be rude to keep refusing her gracious offer so I nod finally. Namrata and Mini both get up.

'We're coming too,' Namrata says.

'No, you guys stay,' I insist but they shake their heads. I thank Hrishita profusely and we all hurry downstairs. While Hrishita coordinates with her driver, I call Amrita and tell her to manage the show and make sure everyone gets a cab. I instruct her to inform Arvind about what's happened. Thankfully, she agrees meekly, maybe because she knows Arvind has a lot riding on this party and she needs to impress him if she has any hope of getting a job in the HR department.

Once we're in the plush car, Mini seems to realize something and puts her head in her hands.

'What's happened?' I ask her, although I really can't stop thinking about Irshad. Please don't let him die, I pray fervently.

Mini shakes her head and gulps. 'This stupid car,' she whispers. Uh oh. Akash's car. Namrata raises an eyebrow questioningly. Fine time for her to become a tube light again.

'The long drives . . . picnic in Nandi Hills,' she whispers. 'And . . . we even did it here, on the back seat, once.'

Um. TMI. Namrata looks away embarrassed.

I put my arm around Mini. 'You're leaving all this behind. What does it matter now?'

Mini looks up. 'I was a fool. Such a fool to believe all that he said.' Namrata and I try to console her for the rest of the ride, making small talk to keep our minds off our pressing issues. The only interruption is when my phone rings and I look at it frantically, worried that it is Farida again.

'It's Vinay,' I tell no one in particular, as I answer the call.

'Hey! What happened? Where did all of you go?' he asks. I fill him in on all the details.

'You guys won't believe what happened,' he says, sounding excited. I put him on speakerphone. 'Akash's wife slapped him. In front of everyone. And then she walked away, saying she's leaving him for good.'

Wow!

'Arvind was so shocked, but all he wanted to know was if Hrishita was going to work with the company,' he continues.

'What did she say?'

'She gave him this look. Like how one would look at a cockroach. She said yes, she still plans on working at Citron because she's going to divorce her husband and will need to be financially independent. You should have seen Akash's face! And Arvind's for that matter.'

Mini doesn't say anything but just looks straight ahead.

'Err . . . is Namrata with you guys?' he asks when there's silence at our end.

'Yes,' Namrata says.

Taking pity on Vinay, I switch off the speakerphone and hand my mobile to Namrata. It's mostly a one-sided conversation with him talking and her listening, apart from saying, 'no' and 'yes' a couple of times.

'Okay, I'll see you then,' she says and hands the phone back to me.

'What was that all about?' I ask her. Mini is lost in her own thoughts.

'He wanted to know if we were coming back. I said no. He said he wanted to come to the hospital too. I told him it was okay,' she says. Clearly, she's not telling us everything. But I can't think of questioning her further because we've arrived.

I thank Hrishita's driver and ask him to leave.

We find Farida outside the emergency ward, a streak of blood on her kurta, her eyes frantic and a little mad. She spots us and runs towards me, enveloping me in a hug, breaking down loudly. I rub her back, the nervous tension gathering in my body, and look up to see Ajay.

'What's happening? How is he?' I ask them.

'They're attending to him now. We don't know anything yet,' Ajay says, sounding sombre. I lick my dry lips, willing my breathing to slow down. Farida is clinging to me and crying.

'He's not going to die,' I tell her firmly and she wipes her face with the back of her hand.

'I fought with him. I told him to leave and never come back. I mean . . . it's all so silly now. I felt he was being patronizing, telling me how I felt, that I was just infatuated with him and not in love with him. It made me so mad that I yelled at him. He was supposed to leave later but he left then . . . and . . .' she breaks off, crying.

'Look, if he'd left later and Ajay hadn't been around, it could have been worse. So maybe it's all for the best,' I tell her.

Farida begins to pace and I look at her nervously. The others have found seats. Mini seems to have completely lost her buzz and just stares at her hands.

Finally, a doctor emerges and we all rush to him. 'He's going to be fine,' he says and we all collectively exhale in relief. Most of his words rush over me—injury, needs to be under observation, blood loss, admitted. Farida is crying hard as she holds on to me.

'Can we see him?' I ask. The doctor nods. 'Just one person at a time please.'

Farida goes in and returns a little while later, bursting into tears. 'He's alive. He's fine,' she mumbles.

I go in and see that they're getting ready to shift him to the ward. He's conscious, and I linger around only for a bit, not sure what to say to him except ask how he's feeling. He gives me a small smile, but he's obviously in pain. Outside, Farida is finally sitting down with Mini and Namrata, sobbing again.

'He shouldn't have come to Bangalore. None of this would have happened,' she says, wiping her eyes. I crouch down before her and lift her chin.

'There's no point in crying about what should or should not have happened. This is it. It's happened. He's fine. Everything will be fine,' I tell her firmly. Where has Ajay disappeared to? Then I spot him speaking to two policemen, who approach us cautiously.

'I called the police. Those men need to be arrested,' Ajay says grimly.

The police ask Farida some questions and then leave, saying they will be back to talk to Irshad once he's better. Just as they are leaving, Vinay joins us.

'Is there anything you guys need me to do? I'm here for any running around,' he says as he sits down on a plastic chair near Namrata.

'Thanks,' I tell him. Farida seems distracted and worried as just then orderlies wheel Irshad out on a stretcher and quickly take him towards the lift. Farida breaks into a sprint and follows them, stopping right near the stretcher. I follow her warily.

Irshad's head is bandaged and he doesn't look as terrible as he did in the emergency ward where his clothes were torn and bloody and I could see several bruises which are now hidden under a sheet.

'I'm so sorry,' she says.

'For what?' he mumbles. The lift doors open and the orderlies wheel him inside.

'Go,' I nudge her and she follows them uncertainly.

'Don't do this again! Ever,' Farida says just as the lift doors close. I can't hear Irshad's reply but the last thing I see as the doors close is his hand reaching out to hold Farida's.

53

Farida calls me a while later from the ward to say she's spending the night at the hospital with Irshad. Just then, Ajay walks up behind me and places his hand on my shoulders. I feel exhausted.

'Hey,' he whispers.

'Hey,' I turn around and smile a little.

'What now?'

'Where's Anya?'

'At her grandparents'. I told you that, right?' he says. I nod. Can you blame me for forgetting? So much has happened since this morning when he walked in with chocolate cake.

Vinay and Namrata come over. 'Irshad is going to be fine. Farida is staying here with him tonight,' I tell them. I look at their changed dynamics and feel a surge of pride towards Namrata. 'You two head back. Take Mini with you as well.'

Vinay looks down a little awkwardly. 'I came on my bike actually,' he says. Oh. Poor Mini is already a third wheel.

'So, we're off then,' Vinay says. I share a look with Namrata as Vinay reaches out to hold her hand.

'You should go home and rest. I'll come to the hospital first thing in the morning and relieve Farida,' he adds.

'Thanks, Vinay. That's sweet of you,' I tell him. I glance at Mini, who is sitting on one of the hard plastic chairs, looking into the distance. Vinay and Namrata leave together and I make my way to her.

'Have Vinay and Namrata left? I'll go home too,' she says, getting up.

'How? You don't have your car,' I remind her.

She shrugs. 'I'll get an Uber,' she says. 'I don't know where Vinay is taking Namrata and frankly, although I'm happy for her, I don't think I can stand seeing happy people at the moment.'

'Listen . . .'

She cuts me off. 'Priya, thanks for being with me today. But I've made up my mind. Hrishita may not be the bitch I thought she was but I still can't work for her. It's just too weird. I'm emailing my resignation to Arvind now,' she says, pulling out her phone and tapping away.

'Thanks for everything,' she says, hugging me impulsively as I try to hold back tears. Why does this feel like goodbye? 'I'd been alone for so long, I didn't realize what it meant to have friends like you guys.'

'Stay in touch, okay?' I tell her, stepping back.

'You follow my dad on Instagram, so you'll know where I am,' she says, smiling a little. 'Tell Farida that everything will be fine with Irshad. I'm sure they'll work it out.' She walks away, head held up proudly.

Finally, it's just Ajay and me in the emergency waiting room.

'Shall we go?' he asks. I want to first check in on Farida and Irshad before I leave so I head upstairs, accompanied by Ajay.

Irshad is in a private room and Farida is on the attendant's bed, looking at him with utter concentration. His painkillers and sedatives have kicked in so he's asleep. She looks up at me when I enter and gets up to hug me.

'You go home now,' she whispers.

'What about you? Have you eaten? You need a change of clothes.'

'I'm glad you told him how I felt about him,' she says, ignoring my questions.

'What?'

'Yeah. I've had a lot of time to think. I'm glad you said it because now he knows my feelings for him.'

'And why isn't it awkward any more?' I ask, genuinely puzzled.

'He knows how I feel about him. Life is short and anything could have happened to him this evening. Almost losing him has opened my eyes. I'm going to fight for him,' she says.

'You mean you're going to move to Mumbai?' I frown. She shakes her head.

'Before we started fighting, he was telling me that he always wanted to set up a clinic for children but didn't have the resources. I've been thinking we can convert a part of my house into a clinic for him,' she says, her eyes shining.

I'm tired but Farida's words make me want to hit my head against a wall. What part of 'engaged to be married' doesn't she get? I need support and I look around to realize it's only Ajay. He doesn't have the faintest idea what to say in a situation like this, so he just stays quiet.

I exhale loudly. 'Wow! Okay. Have you considered he might bring his wife to live here as well?' I ask. Farida's face clouds over and she shakes her head.

'He's not married. Not yet,' she says. Before I can tell her she really needs to consider Irshad's thoughts on this, he groans slightly and we both look at him.

Farida's face turns pink, wondering if he's heard her.

'I had no idea you'd do all this for attention,' Farida says quietly, standing by his bedside. Irshad opens his eyes and winces. His face is puffy and there are bruises and cuts everywhere.

'Call home,' he says. Farida frowns.

'Mumbai,' he whispers. Farida's nostrils flare up as she understands. 'My phone . . .'

I look at Farida, feeling distressed on her behalf. He obviously wants us to call and tell his fiancée about what has happened. What was Farida thinking? That she could just kidnap him and keep him here forever?

She looks straight ahead. 'Okay. I'll call and tell her,' she says.

'Now,' he whispers. Ajay rummages in his pockets and pulls out Irshad's phone.

'Here, I took it when I chased those goons away,' he says. Farida takes the phone distastefully.

'Shall I talk to her?' I ask but she shakes her head. She turns around so she won't have to face us and dials her number. She talks in a low voice to the woman who holds Irshad's heart. I can see the slump in her shoulders as she ends the call.

'She's coming to Bangalore,' Farida informs Irshad who almost looks relieved. God, I wonder how that's going to play out. Irshad slips back into sleep and I squeeze Farida's hand.

'Look . . .'

She stops me. 'Save the spiel. I know what you're going to say.'

I shrug. 'Look at it this way. At least he's going to be around for a little while longer.'

She exhales loudly and nods. 'Go home. Have fun with what's left of your birthday,' she says. I look at her and then at Irshad. There's nothing left for me to do here.

54

Ajay and I make our way back to his car in silence. My head is spinning with all the things that have happened today. I lean my head back as he starts the car and fall asleep almost instantly.

'We're here,' he says after what feels like just a minute.

Huh? I look around in the darkened basement and get out.

'How did we get here so fast?'

'There wasn't any traffic and you were out like a light,' he says wryly. We walk to the lift side by side.

'I'm so glad you were there today to help out Farida,' I tell him as the lift groans its way to our floor.

He shrugs. 'Just luck, I guess. The police are confident they'll catch this man. Why did he do it though?'

I tell him about Irshad punching Reshma Phuppu's husband.

'I swear I've never seen so much drama in my life,' he muses.

It's true. 'We too haven't seen as much drama,' I counter lightly.

The lift stops and I notice Ajay looks the slightest bit fidgety.

'Go ahead. I'll change and come over. We need to talk,' I tell him.

'Don't change, I mean unless it's uncomfortable or something. I love how you look in this,' he claims, as I pull out my keys from my bag. 'And are we just going to talk?'

I shrug. I honestly don't know.

I drop my keys back inside and together we enter his apartment. The light in the corner throws a warm and intimate glow across the room.

Ajay massages my shoulders and I turn around to find myself in his arms. We kiss, slowly at first, his hands running down my back slowly, sensually. All the events of the day fall away one by one until there's only this. I step in closer and he tightens his grip, moving on to kiss my neck, his hands moving to the zipper at the back.

'Bedroom?' he pants, nipping my neck, and I shake my head. He stops and looks at me, confused. It's finally happening. We're here alone without Anya or Farida or drama and, ideally, I should just shut up and follow his lead, but I can't . . . not until we talk.

'We need to clear up something,' I move away from him and switch on the other lights.

'What is it?' His face is flushed and he's breathing heavily. I'm quite sure I look the same way. My hair is tousled and I want nothing more than to rush back into his arms. It feels like my body is a magnet, being invisibly drawn to him. But, I need this sorted out first. I need to know.

I take a deep breath. 'You told me that you felt safe displaying Kirti's photo. I need you to explain that to me,' I tell him, glancing at the photo. It still pains me slightly.

'Now?' he asks, almost incredulously. I cross my arms and nod. Magnet, stop acting up now, I tell my body.

Sighing, he walks over, picks up the photo and holds it in his hand, looking at it pensively for a while. I look at him worried. Is this how our relationship, or whatever this is, ends? Because I asked him a tough question and he doesn't want to answer? Or because he doesn't know the answer?

As usual, I've jumped to conclusions. He takes a deep breath.

'All these years, I didn't display any of her photos because it hurt too much.'

I look at the photograph. They really had been a perfect family.

'But now, for the first time, I've felt like it is safe because I don't feel pain or even guilt. Her photo reminds me of what I had and what I lost, and that doesn't make me feel panicky inside.'

I look up at him, trying to understand what it must have been like for him to lose her like that.

'I'm okay with it now,' he says, looking at me, his gaze intense. 'It means I'm not afraid of falling in love again.'

There's a kind of endearing earnestness to his voice as he speaks. I look into his face, at the man who has been through so much and still manages to be funny and quirky, at the love he showers on Anya . . . at the love he's willing to shower on me.

I snuggle against him and stroke his arm and he brings it around to hold me tightly as he places the frame back on the table.

'Will Natasha be a problem?' I ask, looking up at his face as he rubs circles on my back.

'She's the last person I'm thinking of right now,' he says in a low voice.

'Typical. Guys just can't multitask,' I joke.

'I hope you're not thinking of anyone else right now either,' he says, a warning tone in his voice.

I sigh and he holds me tighter. I've always found it amazing how we seem to fit in the right places. 'No. But I'm just thinking about my friends and all the different ways their lives are turning out and—'

He gently places a finger on my lips. 'And how is *your* life turning out?' he asks.

I recall Amrita's stunned face today and can't help but grin. 'Splendidly, actually!'

'Splendidly. I like the sound of that. Can we *do* something more splendid now?' he asks, nuzzling my neck.

I put my arms around his neck and lean into him. 'Maybe.'

Thank god, a thirtieth birthday comes just once in a lifetime.

Epilogue

Obviously my mother has found out that Ajay and I are together and is planning to come over soon to 'finalize' things.

'What does she mean by that? What does "finalize" mean?' I squeak when I read her text. Ajay who is curled up next to me on the sofa, while we watch a movie, only grins.

'Let her come. We'll deal with her,' he says, leaning in close to kiss me.

'Anya!' I have to remind him furiously.

'Asleep,' he assures me, but I am not convinced. 'Fine, I'll go check.'

Farida has moved back to her house and Irshad is living with her while he recovers. The police caught Reshma Phuppu's husband and the other men, and that matter has been put to rest. Irshad's fiancée, of course, arrived the very next day and there has been such an undercurrent of tension between the three of them.

I hated Irshad's fiancée on first sight, obviously because I'm biased. But Shagufta isn't very nice either. She blamed the entire incident on Farida, saying none of this would have

239

happened if he hadn't come to Bangalore. Irshad didn't agree and backed Farida up, saying she was his cousin and family and that she needed him, which made Shagufta hate Farida even more, I guess.

Farida also doesn't make things easy for her. She regularly drops huge hints about her plan for the house, tempting Irshad with ideas for the children's clinic. Shagufta was aghast that Irshad was even considering it, and they have had a few arguments in front of Farida, with Shagufta threatening to call off the engagement if he so much as thinks of moving to Bangalore.

'It will take just a nudge,' Farida told me over the phone, sounding rather happy. I frowned.

'Don't manipulate the situation, Farida,' I told her. 'I feel bad for Irshad. He shouldn't have to choose between her and the clinic.'

'Don't you mean between me and her?' she asked. I sighed. Maybe one of these days Irshad will see her differently, but I think she is just digging a hole for herself from which she will emerge Irshad-less.

'Don't become a Hindi serial vamp,' I reminded her.

'Ha ha,' she cackled, sounding rather like one of the sari-clad women in spaghetti strap blouses, over-the-top make-up and arched eyebrows who make conniving plans involving other women's husbands.

'I'm serious,' I told her and she sobered up.

'I know. I won't do anything. I'm just showing him what life will be like if he chooses to stay here. That's all,' she said. I didn't believe her entirely but that's another story. Although,

I am secretly rooting for her, whether it means being with Irshad or finally moving on.

Mini has moved to Hong Kong and now lives with her father. She's right. I am able to follow her around on his Instagram and she messages me every now and then. She's writing her big novel and seems quite excited about it.

People in the office can't seem to get over Vinay and Namrata getting together. Even the HR manager, her relative, tried to talk to Namrata once and got shot down.

'But your mother! What will she say?'

'She can say what she wants to me. You don't have to worry about her,' Namrata replied calmly.

Akash and Hrishita got divorced. Hrishita is a real sweetheart and has taken Mini's place in our lives, strangely enough. She might be tough to work with but since we're on different teams, we've only seen her caring, friendly side. Her baby is due next month and we're doing all we can to help her before she goes on maternity leave.

Natasha decided to do a business course and went to the UK, leaving Ajay, Anya and me to get to know each other better. And like I said earlier, my mom is coming over. To *finalize* things.

'You're going to get frown lines,' Ajay admonishes me, walking back to the sofa after making sure Anya is in bed. He puts his arm around me and I snuggle up next to him.

'I don't care. Do you?' I ask, looking up at him. He gently strokes the lines on my forehead with his thumb but shakes his head.

I run my fingers through his hair and bring his face close to mine to kiss him lightly. 'I don't know why people go around hiding the obvious signs of ageing with Botox injections and hair dye. You look sexy with your salt-and-pepper hair. It shows that you've lived. You look experienced and I think that's amazing. Have I told you how sexy it is?' I say.

'Priya, I can spot a couple of grey strands on your head too. We can be a matching-matching couple,' he says.

I immediately run to the bathroom to check, his laughter ringing in my ears.

Acknowledgements

Thank you, Penguin Random House, for publishing this book!

I would also like to thank:

My brother, Junaid, for reading this book in its earliest version and telling me that it was nothing like what I'd written until now, and making me believe in this book.

My friends, who have read this book over its different iterations and still loved it—Trisha, Shweta (the Commit gang).

Pooja Premnath, who let me happily dig her brain for all her work-related information (you still have to read it, girl!).

My editor, Roshini, who believed in the book and gave it a chance, and worked on it diligently in every aspect.

Everyone at Penguin Random House who worked on the book—the cover, the copy edits, proofing, etc.

Thank you all!

Lastly, thanks to Allah for making me a writer and letting me live so many different lives.